The Talking Dog Says

For my friend Doug
M.A. Kellogg
8/1/12

Copyright © 2012 Michael A. Kelley
All rights reserved.

ISBN: 1-4681-1039-X
ISBN-13: 9781468110395

The Talking Dog Says

Michael A. Kelley

2012

Dedication

For Petra and Marilou: friends, mentors, and all around good eggs

It had been a really lousy day. My sister was having trouble with her live-in boyfriend, mostly because he's a no good Hole of a man. A drunken, whoring gambler who likes beating women- a real peach. Kathleen had called me in tears. They had had a fight that afternoon, and he had thankfully passed out. Now, he was waking up and she was afraid. Hung over, he was even meaner.

Entering their apartment, I found Steve standing over Kathleen and slapping the hell out of her. He didn't bother to stop or even glance my way. I grabbed him by the hair, pulling him off of her. Whacking him over the head with my 38 Special—you have to be careful hitting someone with a gun, too hard and it's curtains. I hit him just right, instantly subduing him. He went down, but not out. He sat there, stunned, looking at me sourly.

I reached down, grabbing him by the neck and half lifted, half dragged his sorry, abusive ass into a chair. He tried to struggle, but stopped when I raised the gun again.

"Stay there," I ordered, then turned to check on Kathleen. She was sitting on the sofa weeping, and dabbing at her eyes with tissue. Her left eye was swelling, turning purple black. Her bottom lip was double its normal size.

"I'm not hurt," she whispered, a hand over her mouth.

"Like hell you aren't. Kathy, this can't go on."

Steve started to get out of his chair. I turned, pushed him back down. He wasn't much of a man. Close to six feet, but thin; not a developed muscle in his entire body. Big enough to knock around an average-sized woman, but a complete wimp otherwise. "I'm not done with you." I grabbed a handful of his right cheek, and shook him back and forth by his face- it's a nice demeaning show of force.

He didn't have a whole lot of strength to fight back- beating a woman a third your size must take a lot of energy.

I turned him loose. "Steve, you're moving out. You and Kathy are splitting up as of this second." I nudged him. "Get moving. Pack your crap up and get out."

He sat there, an especially dumb, vacant look on his face, as if he didn't understand. I leaned down next to him. His cheek was red, and already bruising from my little massage. I grabbed the end of his cheesy mustache, and tugged. "This is it, Steve. It's over." He looked past me at Kathleen. She'd been dabbing at her eyes, looked up to see his best sad, sorry-assed imploring look.

"Knock it off," I told him. "She's not your mother."

Kathy wasn't buying it either. "Get out, Steve," she said, quietly. She stood, and went into the bathroom. He wanted to follow, but I took him by the arm. "You've got two minutes to get what you need. Pack!" Steve sighed, changing his course, to the bedroom.

"You're a real jerk, Jim," he told me. "I just want to..."

"It's too late. Now get to it."

Ten minutes later I found him sitting on the bed, looking dejected. He hadn't made any attempt to do anything.

"Oh, for Christ's sake!" I took him by the arm. He tried to shake loose, so I twisted his arm behind him, led him to the hallway door. I leaned him, face first, into the wall. "You let me: get it Steve? Let *me* know where to send your stuff. Don't call her. Don't come back here. Leave her alone, or I swear..." I turned him around so he could see me. "I swear, I'll put this gun so far up your rectum you'll be hiccoughing gunpowder. You got that?

"Yes. I'll leave her alone, Jim. I promise." His promises had proven to be completely worthless. I opened the hall door, pushed him out of the apartment.

"Call my office when you know where you end up. I'll see your stuff is sent." I slammed the door shut.

Kathleen came out of the bathroom. "Is he gone?"

The Talking Dog Says

"Are you alright, Kathy?"

"Y-yeah." Her lip quivered. "I can't believe that asshole!"

"Hon, come sit down." We sat on the sofa. I touched her cheek below her swelling eye. Time to be firm with her: "Kathy, this can't go on. You've got to do something to help yourself. If you let him back into your life again he's going to maim or kill you. "

"I know. I know. It's just…"

"It's Just nothing, Kathy. You need to get a restraining order. You need some professional help. I want you to go to Family Services."

She didn't respond. She knew I was right, but the bastard had his hooks in her. "Okay Jim," she said, finally, her eyes filling up with tears all over again. "Should I call the police now?"

"Yes, do it. I'll wait till they get here, but be sure to tell them he's gone, and your brother is with you."

She managed to smile. "You don't want to be mistaken for him?"

"Some of those guys despise me since I left the Job and got my P.I. license. They'd likely beat my head in before any explanations could be made."

"Stop showing them up, Jim," she said. "You made them look silly more than once."

I had become a private investigator after serving four years as a Minneapolis police officer. On the force, I'd been a successful officer with good reviews. I'd been on the fast track to getting a Detective's shield. I'd been included on a couple of interviews, and had gained some confessions that hadn't been, by any means, a certainty. I gained a reputation for breaking down people's defenses, and getting what we wanted out of them.

The problem was I just couldn't tolerate having a dozen bosses, and all the mindless rules and paperwork. It's disturbing how difficult it is to put a serial killer, or even a drunk driver, behind bars. It seemed like each day someone was telling me I'd done something incorrectly. One day, I said 'enough' and walked out.

I formally resigned to form The Diamond Agency, a modest one-man shop that had immediately found enough success to keep business coming in the door. Most of it was small town, small time, but I had taken on a double murder case that had gone cold with the local police. After discovering that the murderer was probably Michael Roy Greene, by finding and unraveling the breakthrough clues, I had located and captured Greene one scary breath-taking night.

I had followed a hunch. Michael Greene had been the victim; Anthony Cochran's roommate in college, twenty years earlier. They hadn't seen each other in all that time, but they had parted company acrimoniously, a fact that the police had never noticed, or just didn't go back far enough to discover. Greene had never been interviewed after Cochran and his girlfriend Jessica were brutally murdered.

Greene, it turned out, was a rich boy who had all of life's amenities handed to him from the moment of his birth. He did anything he wanted to do and if there were repercussions, money and political influence straightened it out. I discovered old newspaper clippings detailing his arrest as a nine-year-old child, for cruelty to animals; usually birds, frogs, and other little creatures that couldn't defend themselves. It's a big red flag for a serial killer.

When Michael Greene's parents were killed in a small airplane accident in 2001, he was lavished with sympathy and pity, and no one thought about his problems. Michael didn't waste too much time grieving, however. He traveled for a time, but came back to their palatial home on Lake Minnetonka, and abruptly sold it. Not long after, he just disappeared from the public view and was soon forgotten.

When I connected him to Tony Cochran, I pored over all the public records, and began visiting anyone who had

The Talking Dog Says

ever known Michael Greene. No one knew where he was, and no one cared much either. In a true stroke of luck, I one day noticed a reference to a family cabin in the estate papers, but I never found anything that told me the cabin had ever left Michael Green's possession. I didn't have an address. It was described as a small log affair somewhere in the Northern Minnesota woods, just south of the Canadian border, somewhere near Thief River Falls. I went up there, looking like Paul Bunyan, and began combing the small towns and communities that punctuate the wilderness. It took me three weeks on the road to discover even one person who had ever known Michael Greene.

A stereotypical Minnesotan with red suspenders on green jeans, and a bright-colored flannel shirt; he owned a small supply and grocery store in the absolute middle of nowhere. All he knew was that Greene had frequented his place for years, and 'reckoned' that his cabin was somewhere out 'thataway,' which narrowed it down to fifty miles in any direction, but started in the direction he pointed.

Another man, a frequent hunter, told me of a cabin deep in the woods, that had been there since he was a child. He remembered the owners were 'hoity toity' people, who had cut a foot path through the woods so that their hiking wasn't hampered by such an ignoble thing as nature. He said that he hadn't seen them in years, but knew that someone was staying in the cabin. The path, he said, though still there, had grown over and started to disappear.

The cabin, it turned out, was about four football fields into the woods, and still took a decent amount of effort to get to. I navigated it slowly, careful not to fall and twist an ankle, or make too much noise. Likely, if Greene had murdered two people in their home, he'd have no qualms about killing me in the middle of fricking nowhere.

It was mid-afternoon when I reached the cabin. It was in a small clearing with a tool shed and very little else. I walked the perimeter, staying several yards in the woods.

I was wearing camouflage, and especially in the waning light, felt reasonably sure that I would not be spotted from the cabin. Unfortunately, it didn't appear that anyone was there. With all the trees blocking the sun, it was dark, and though I knew he couldn't have electricity, I figured he had kerosene lamps and flashlights- possibly a gas generator. I waited several hours, protected from most of the bugs by very strong spray. The place gave every appearance of being totally deserted.

Finally, brave soul that I am, I crept up to the cabin and peered through a window. Not a single light or sound. I tried the door, and was only momentarily surprised when it opened. He probably didn't worry too much about intruders or burglars this far in the boondocks, but with his money, he probably felt he could replace just about anything.

I lit a match, shielding it with my hand, just in case he came back suddenly. Stupid thing to do, I guess. He'd have instantly smelled the match whether he saw it or not. I had my trusty .38 with me, and was ready for any surprises. None came. He obviously wasn't here, but a quick check of the cabin told me that he was staying here. There was fresh bread on the counter, and wood piled up by a stove in the center of the main room.

I could have gone back to civilization and come back with the police. I could have gone and come back myself; but I decided I would just camp out in his living room, and wait for him to return. Hopefully, it would be before I became too tired. I decided if that happened, I would retreat to the woods, on the far side from the path, for the night. I didn't want the murdering bastard finding me asleep. I knew I wouldn't ever wake up again if that happened.

What do you do when you're in a cabin in the middle of nowhere, sitting in the dark, and waiting for a killer to return so you can arrest him? I kept alert, thinking about anything, and everything that came to mind. I thought about each person I knew, friends, enemies, lovers. I spent a lot of time thinking about my current lady friend, Marian. She didn't think much of policemen or private detectives, but we were pretty nuts about each other, and had a lot of fun together. After thinking of damn near everyone in my life, I switched to song.

I knew, by heart, every record album Arlo Guthrie ever recorded, and I began singing them in my mind. When I finished with Arlo, I switched to the Beatles. I was somewhere in the middle of "Rubber Soul", when I heard sticks crunching outside. I sat up in the chair and took out the .38. The door opened slowly, and a figure came in, only enough light left outside to see him in the doorway. This being so, he left the door stand open, and went to the kitchen table. He scratched a match, carefully lit the lamp, set it back on the table. He turned around to close the door, and found me pointing my gun at his heart.

"Hi Michael. How's tricks." He was a big guy, about twice my size, and he looked intently at the gun. "Don't even think about it Mike. It's loaded, and I'll put three in you before you can get to me."

"Who the hell are you? What do you want? I haven't got anything to steal."

"I know Mike. You live really frugal for such a rich man. What's that about? Are you a little goofy, or is it just part of your hiding strategy."

"Hiding? What the hell do I have to hide about? I've been living up here for years. I like the solitude."

"Yeah, I'll bet you do, Mike. Let's talk about how you killed Anthony and Jessica in cold blood." He shuddered, and took a step back. "Yeah, now you know why I'm here. I've come to arrest you for killing your college roommate and his girlfriend. That's why you're hiding, you big shithead."

"You got nothing. Who the hell are you anyway? You can't just break into my place and accuse me of killing someone."

"Oh, but I can, Mike. Door was open, and I was afraid something had happened to you. You don't call. You don't write. What could I do but check on you, up here in the middle of nowhere all alone."

"I didn't kill anyone. You don't have anything on me."

"The police will get it out..." That's when he made his move. He leaped toward the table, grabbing the lit kerosene lamp, heaving it at me. I ducked, and it sailed over me into the wall of his cabin, exploding into a wall of flame. I moved away at the same time shooting at him as he raced out the cabin door. I followed, but he was waiting for me and punched me in the face harder than I've ever been punched. I went down and my gun went off again, catching him in the thigh. He screamed and went down beside me, where we wrestled and fought for the gun.

I didn't want to shoot him again, and had to worry about getting him out of the woods before he croaked, so I jammed the gun barrel into the wound I'd just put in his thigh. He screamed madly, then passed out from the pain. I had brought along rope with my supplies, and I quickly tied him up hog style, all the time bleeding out of my nose. Only when he was safely trussed up could I attend to myself, before treating his leg.

Praying there would be a telephone signal, I opened my cell phone, and dialed 911. Lucky for Michael, I got through. "I've apprehended a suspect in a double murder. He's injured. I'm in the middle of the woods northeast of Thief River Falls, and the cabin is on fire. You'll have to use my phone signal, and the flames to find us."

Michael was a pretty unhappy camper, tied up like a pig, and waiting to be taken to prison for the rest of his life. I probably didn't help his mood, having nothing else to do but question his murdering ass. "Why did you do it? Why did you kill your college buddy and his girlfriend. You hadn't seen him in almost twenty years, Mike."

"Go to hell."

The Talking Dog Says

"No, you'll be the one making that trip, Mike. Come on, tell me. Why? Could you possibly have held some varsity grudge for all that time? Or maybe he stole a girl from you long ago, and you just couldn't get over her ass. That it, Mike?"

"Please stop, you stupid sonofabitch. I'm not going to admit anything to you. You can kiss my fat bleeding ass."

"Well it is fat, Mike; but it's not bleeding.

Not lucky for Michael, however, they didn't find us until morning. I managed to get some sleep, but mostly watched his cabin burn, sincerely praying that it didn't spread to the woods. I moved myself and my prisoner upwind, and felt safe. Michael, was quite senseless and delusional by then, and in urgent need of medical care.

They found us just after dawn, but could not land the helicopter anywhere useful. They ended up tying Michael Greene into an evac basket and lifting him above the trees, giving him an aerial ride back to the highway, where they could set him down next to a waiting ambulance. I walked back out of the woods, with a police escort, which it turned out, was just as much to keep me in custody, as lead me back to civilization. The whole thing in the middle of nowhere was a lot for the locals to digest very quickly. I was taken back to Thief River Falls for a statement.

I had to explain the whole mess to the guys in the local sheriff's office who were just as willing to arrest me for attempted murder as look into Michael Roy Greene. In the end, they did let me go, and locked up the right fellow. Looking into the facts, the authorities came to the conclusion that I had captured the murderer of Anthony Cochran and Jessica Daniels.

Then, full of drama, Greene confessed in mid-trial to the murders. It turned out that Cochran and he had gotten into an argument about Greene's inherited wealth back in their college days, and Cochran, being a bit of a snob and asshole his own self, shot his mouth off that rich people deserved to die young so that their wealth could be used for something constructive.

Fifteen years later, when Greene's parents were killed, he could not stop thinking about the comment, and let it eat him up inside until he hunted his former roommate down and murdered him and his companion. I've said it before, and I'll say it again: Not counting psychotic crazies, whose reasons can be quite abstract and bizarre, it doesn't take much for someone prone to murder, to want to kill someone else, and it seems, the more horrific the death count, the stupider the reasons for it.

I had realized that this case was going to make me enemies in the Department, and had turned my hog-tied prisoner over to the police, who promptly shipped him back to the Minneapolis authorities, who reported the arrest to the media without mentioning any involvement by me or my Agency. The truth, of course, came out during the trial. The press was especially hard on the police for taking all the credit, and I became a bit of a local hero.

I never gave a single interview regarding Greene. Nor did I, as far as I can remember, ever rub their faces in it. I suppose, though, that they assumed I cut a lot of legal corners to get the results I got: that I used methods that they never could do without legal repercussions. All of that was probably true. I had no qualms about this or that, if it got me to where I wanted to be; but I'd always been careful to keep the authorities in the loop.

So, Kathleen was half right. I had, at times, outshined my former brothers in blue, but hadn't done anything to promote it, and done all I could to prevent their enmity, a fact that went almost completely unacknowledged by the Minneapolis Police Department.

After the evening with Steve and Katherine, I limped home, exhausted physically and mentally. I showered, then collapsed into my recliner with a bottle of Zinfandel. It didn't take long to polish it off, and I was half asleep when I heard

The Talking Dog Says

something bump against my front door. Then, the door rattled like it was being shaken. I pushed the footrest of the chair down to the floor, stood up. Steve, I thought. What is that crazy bastard doing now?

With a loud crash the door was busted in. It slammed against the wall and back toward the intruder.

"Jesus Christ!" I heard a man stage whisper. "You wanna wake up the whole damn block."

"Shut up," hissed a second intruder. "Give me that flashlight."

A light beam cut through the darkness, and though it couldn't bend around the corner to where I was, it did provide just enough light for me to see the empty wine bottle laying on the floor at my feet. My gun, in its belt, was across the room from where I was standing. If I tried to reach it they'd hear me.

Silently, I picked up the bottle by its neck and waited. 'Jesus Christ', the first man to enter my home, came around the corner holding the flashlight in one hand and a huge Glock in the other. I whacked him right on the chin with the empty Zinfandel bottle. He never knew what hit him. He stumbled forward, collapsing with hardly a sound.

The second man thought his buddy had tripped. He laughed. "You clumsy..." He didn't finish the thought. The bottle connected with his nose. Unlike his friend, he screamed in pain, tried to retreat, but I hit him alongside the head with a fist. He fell on top of the first man, groaning and bleeding.

I flipped on the hall light to get a better look. Neither man was Steve- both were much too big. I searched their pockets, removing wallets, careful to stay away from the blood. I found a second Glock and set both of their semi-automatic toys safely aside, thinking about what nice big holes they'd have made in me, or whatever else they hit.

A cellphone began ringing- and it wasn't mine. I pulled the top burglar onto his side, and listened. The ring was coming from the first man's pocket, and I removed the phone. It was playing "Fifty Ways to Leave Your Lover."

Hit him with a jug, Doug.

I opened the cellphone. Grunted, "Yeah."

"Harry? Harry? You sound funny."

"Bad connection," I mumbled.

"Is it done?"

"Steve, is that you?" It didn't sound like him at all, but I was playing a hunch.

"Steve?" The voice was puzzled. "Who in the world is..." His light came on. The phone went dead.

Closing, then re-opening the phone, I punched in 911. I liked the idea of using the burglars' phone to summon the police. "This is Jim Diamond. My house has been invaded... No. No, they're still here. I had to subdue them, but you better get someone over here...ambulance too."

A black and white pulled up just ahead of the paramedics. Two officers, both in need of a better fitness plan, huffed and puffed up the sidewalk. I pushed the broken front door out of their way.

"Geezus, Diamond!" exclaimed one cop, seeing the two bloodied would-be burglars. "Did you kill 'em both?" His name was McLindon. The bulkier of the two, I remembered him well from when I was still a police officer. I once saw his wife bitch-slap him damn near to tears at a Christmas party. It was hard to take him very seriously.

"They were living the last time I checked. Where the hell is the ambulance?"

"There it comes. What happened in here?"

"They broke my door down and threatened me. I could have been killed."

"Hey, we're glad you're okay Jim-o. None of us could sleep again if something was to happen to you." McLindon didn't take me seriously either.

Bennett, his partner was speaking into his shoulder, calling in the condition of the two intruders. When he finished, he turned to me. "Awful lucky you had an empty wine bottle handy." He pointed to two more bottles sitting on my kitchen cabinet. "Looks like you could have taken on a whole battalion!" Then, to McLindon. "Gene, you think a wine bottle could be considered a deadly weapon?"

The paramedics had come and were attending to the injured burglars. One medic pressed a compress against the bleeding nose. "Hold this," he instructed his patient.

"I could have shot them both carrying these," I told the officers, who were doing their best to give me a hard time. I handed the two Glocks to Bennett. "Wouldn't be a judge in the entire state that would convict me. Oh, and here's a cellphone. It rang after I whacked the one that isn't bleeding."

"They both look pretty bloody."

"Yeah, this one bled all over that one," I said, pointing from one to the other.

Bennett took the two weapons and the cell phone. "You *could* have been killed," he admitted looking at the guns.

The paramedics were wheeling the burglars out. Both were awake and responsive, and objecting to how badly they'd been treated. Bennett held a hand up, stopping the caravan. "You're lucky he didn't shoot both of you," he growled. "I would have." Damn, maybe he was on my side. Nothing brings reality to a policeman more than the thought of facing a Glock. He motioned for McLindon to go with the paramedics.

Turning back to me, Bennett said: "Look Jim: it looks like this went down cleanly. Do you have any idea what it's about? Why did they come after you? You in some kind of trouble?"

"I thought I was being burglarized."

Bennett shook his head. "Most common burglars don't carry guns at all. You know that. Come on, you must suspect something."

I weighed the idea of telling them about Steve. If he was guilty, it would end Kathleen's problem. If he was innocent, he'd be released, even angrier and more resentful. Bennett saw the wheels turning, and gave me an impatient look. "Spill it. I can still haul you in, you know."

I sighed. "It's delicate. See, my sister is being abused by her live-in. I found him beating her earlier tonight. I intervened and gave him encouragement to behave more responsibly."

Bennett smirked. He knew what that meant: I'd laid hands on Steve.

"Did you hurt him?"

"I slapped him around a bit. Kicked him out, and told him not to ever come back, or else."

McLindon stuck a forefinger up in the air. "Steve Kruckman, right?"

"You know him?"

"We've been over there a couple of times, Jim. Do you really think he arranged this?"

"No. He didn't have enough time. As big of an asshole as he is, he doesn't hang around with Glock-toting thugs.

"I'd appreciate it if you left Steve out of it until we find out who these guys are, and who sent them. I don't want to give him another reason to hurt Kathleen."

Bennett nodded. "That guy doesn't need a reason, but I hear you. I won't put it in the report...for now."

"Thanks."

He nodded. "Carlson may have questions about all this, Jim. I'd stay close to the phone." He motioned to my bloodstained hallway. "You'll probably be cleaning up blood all day anyway."

Morning arrived quickly. I was all keyed up and couldn't sleep. I had blood to clean up, and a door to get fixed. Cleaning up the blood came first: the longer I waited, the worse it would be. Fortunately, 'Broken Nose' had bled

The Talking Dog Says

more on his buddy, 'Jesus Christ', then he had on my hallway. Likely, the hospital staff had burned all their clothing, and spent a good amount of time cleaning their two new charges. Imagining the both of them being booked in hospital gowns with their asses hanging out made me smile.

Next, I set about repairing the door enough so that I could close it again. I got it properly aligned and hung, and found that if I locked it from the inside, I could go out the back door, and the place would be secure until I could get a locksmith, a carpenter, or both, to fix it properly.

Finally, a little after six a.m., I laid back down, sleeping until eleven. I dragged myself out of bed as drowsy as I've ever felt. Trudging into the kitchen, I set up the coffee, and headed for the bathroom.

The telephone rang as I was dressing. It was Kathleen. "Are you okay?" I asked.

"Yes, Jim. He did what he was told. He hasn't come back."

"Don't count on that for long, Kathy. He's licking his wounds now, but his ego will kick in soon."

"I know," she sighed. "I'm leaving for an appointment with my lawyer and Family Services. I want that restraining order. I can't trust him at all anymore." It had taken a half dozen beatings, and an assortment of bruises, black eyes, and other injuries for her to come to this realization. I was disgusted with her, but also too disgusted with myself to judge her. I should have taken him for a one-way ride a long time ago. By now, Kathleen could have moved on to someone nice, I wouldn't have to be so worried, and Steve's parents would be over his sudden 'suicide.'

After talking with my sister, I checked in with my office girl, Emily Blake. "Morning hon. I'm running a bit late...trouble last night Emmie. I'll fill you in when I get there. Anything to report?" Nothing.

Then, taking some time for myself, I sat down with the Tribune and a cup of coffee. I was on my second cup, contentedly chewing a toasted waffle, when the doorbell rang. Shirtless, coffee cup in hand, I crossed the room and peeked out a front window. It was a couple of Uni's I didn't recognize. I pulled the door open.

"Mr. Diamond? Good morning. Lieutenant Carlson sent us to pick you up."

"What for?" Victor Carlson, the hard-nosed Lieutenant of the Homicide division was a bit of a nemesis. I had turned my big murder case over to him, and he'd gotten the credit for the whole thing. He'd been promoted, and that, I'm sure, was the problem. Not only did he get the glory and a promotion he didn't deserve, he'd been made to look like a fool when the trial revealed my involvement. Worst of all he was stuck in a position that the media portrayed as a mistake. He'd been subjected to a lot of abuse that hadn't been necessary or fair, but on the other hand, he had known he didn't deserve a promotion when it was given to him, and had done nothing.

After quitting the Job for a P.I. license, I was hardly one of the good Lieutenant's favorite people. I didn't really relish going into headquarters to see him. There was no way to predict how he might twist last night's attack.

"He's concerned. The two men that attacked you have thick jackets. He'll tell you all about it."

I checked my pants pocket for my keys and wallet. Picking up my cellphone from the kitchen counter, I turned back to the boys. "Alright, let's go." I locked up the house, exiting from the back door and meeting them out front; and we were off.

The drive downtown from my house only takes a few minutes. My escorts talked to each other, more or less ignoring me, but that was fine. I didn't know either man. Small talk would probably have been brutal. We arrived at the 5th Avenue headquarters in record time, and into the private underground parking ramp. The ride up the elevator was equally lonely.

The Talking Dog Says

Carlson stood as I was ushered into his office. He extended his hand, smiling. "Thank you for coming in, Mr. Diamond. I wanted to talk about that break in. I hear you had a close call last night."

"You heard correctly."

"Well, it was a closer call than you realized."

"Sir?"

"It turns out your two burglars have quite a history." He picked up a folder from his desk. "Now, there's Jack Bickford, who's been arrested for so many vicious shenanigans that we needed another ream of paper for the fax machine. Mr. Bickford has done time for everything from animal cruelty to car theft and armed robbery. He's rumored to have connections to the Jersey mob."

"The Mob!" I couldn't believe that. What could those goons possibly have against me?

"The other man is Harry Carter. Mr. Carter is a stone cold mob assassin. He was nearly convicted of first degree murder, but the witness suddenly decided to take a permanent vacation without telling anyone. The case had to be dropped. He's sought for questioning in three more murder cases, but no one can find him." Carlson took his glasses off, laying them on his desk. "Now tell me, Mr. Diamond: Why is the Mob breaking into the less-than-stately home of a third rate private eye, a thousand miles from home?"

Third rate! "Now Lieu," I said. "They could be from Chicago."

Victor Carlson is a man of little humor. "Don't be a smart ass, Diamond. This is very serious."

"I don't know what to say. I've never..."

"Come on. You know these guys. You knew they were coming."

I shook my head. "No. I haven't ever heard of, or seen either man before. I definitely didn't know they were coming."

"You had a good non-lethal weapon ready. Personally, I wouldn't have taken any chances with these two. You're very lucky to be alive. You should be anchored to the bottom of the Mississippi right now!"

"Lieu, I was half asleep. The wine bottle was right there. My gun was on the other side of the room. If I had tried to reach it, they'd have heard, and shot holes the size of your hand in me."

He thought about that. He pushed a pad of paper toward me. "Show me."

I looked at him, but he was serious: He wanted a diagram. Quickly, I drew out my front door, the hallway into my living room. Setting the pen down, I pushed the pad so we could both see it.

"Here's the door. Here's where I was asleep. I had a little TV tray sitting next to the chair. The wine bottle fell off of it."

"So, you grabbed the wine bottle and waited here?" he asked, pointing.

"Luckily, that worked out. The first guy had a flashlight. I could see him coming, and when he came around the corner, I belted him."

"How did you surprise his buddy?"

"He thought the first guy tripped. He started laughing..."

"If you had missed either one, they'd have killed you."

"I never dreamed they could be carrying major hardware, or be connected. If I had known they were killers, I would have had to make a dive for my gun."

"What are you carrying these days?"

"Thirty-eight."

"They'd have still killed you with those cannons. Damn lucky you're a drinker." He didn't smile. This was as close as he could approach a joke.

"I'd had a rough day. I was relaxing."

"Your sister?"

The Talking Dog Says

Damned Bennett. He promised to keep his mouth shut. No, he had promised to keep quiet until we knew more about my assailants. "Aw yeah. Kathleen."

"You should be relieved that Kruckman had nothing to do with it."

"I'd rather see him in jail, Lieu."

"That's where he is now."

I was alarmed. "Kathy!"

He patted the air. "No, she's okay. She went to Family Services this morning. I was there on another matter, and heard your name mentioned. I asked a few questions, and got the whole story. They and I agreed he should be picked up and charged. Her eye is looking bad this morning."

I was stunned. "I'm grateful Lieutenant, but this could make things worse."

"They're going to take care of her, Mr. Diamond. She's safe."

"And Kruckman?"

"We're going to keep him as long as we can. He can't afford a lawyer, so one is being appointed. We just won't break any speed records doing it."

"It'll only…"

"Listen Diamond: we all have sisters and mothers. Family Service will take care of her. She's got old bruises and injuries. He won't be able to get to her."

They were putting her in a Safe House. "Who knows all this?"

"Next to no one. These matters are taken very seriously. Believe me, she's safe. Just be patient, and wait for her call."

"Thanks. Thanks Lieutenant."

"Now, that that is settled: what are we going to do about you? Someone wants you dead."

I could take care of myself, but I was feeling shaky. "I don't know what to tell you. Do they have a bunk bed wherever they're taking Kathy?"

That annoyed him. Damn, we'd been getting along so well. "Much as you piss me off ninety percent of the time, I can't have you getting shot up. Whoever did this is likely to try again."

"I didn't know you cared, Vic."

"I don't care, and don't call me that," he snarled. "This is just politics, and you might mind your manners. I might decide you'd look good with a couple more holes in your head, and send you home." Now, that was the Victor Carlson we all knew and loved.

"I think it's best that we put a team on you for awhile, Diamond."

An officer appeared at the door. "Lieutenant? We just got a call. There's been a disturbance at Mr. Diamond's office.

Shit! Emmie was there alone. I jumped up. "What kind of disturbance?"

"Shots fired. We're on the way. We'll know more in a few minutes."

I moved to the door. "I've got to get down there."

"Hold it right there, Diamond. You're not going anywhere."

"It's my office! My secretary is down there alone. My God!"

"Let them get the place secured. I don't want you anywhere near there right now. There could still be perps down there waiting for you to show up." He was switching from good to bad cop, and back again so fast I was getting dizzy.

"But..."

"Think about it: They shoot the place up. Who is going to be the first person on the scene? You, that's who...I'll take you down there myself when the coast is clear."

I sat back down, put my head in my hands. "I need to know that she's not hurt, Lieutenant."

"You will. As soon as we get word."

The Talking Dog Says

I clenched my fists. "I want to talk to those two gorillas from last night!"

"We'll discuss that after we know that your staff is safe. Come on. Let's go get a cup of coffee."

The report from my office was grim and unsettling. Carlson told me everything had been destroyed by gunfire. Emily was nowhere to be found. Carlson had a strange look in his eye, and it seemed to me that there was something he wasn't telling me. Whatever it was, it was disturbing this veteran police Lieutenant. That terrified me.

Despite all this: knowing that the Diamond Agency was no more, that Emily was unaccounted for, and that something unspeakable might have happened, I was nevertheless, unprepared for what I found. Carlson finally took me down to the crime scene. The police were everywhere. One might think that Kennedy had just been assassinated. The entire block had been taped off from the street to the line of buildings. Uni's were interviewing witnesses from one end to the other. Plain clothes detectives bustled in and out of the building. I recognized both CSI and Homicide officers. A canine unit arrived, and the handler led the dog into the building.

I followed Carlson under the yellow tape, then into the building. The interior of my flat had been thoroughly raked by an automatic weapon, punctuated by shotgun blasts that had blown holes in the cheaply made walls. I could see into the next room, and in the outer wall, into my neighbor's offices. Anxious and scared faces stared back at me through those holes. The acrid smell of gunpowder was everywhere, and hung in the air like a cloud. Everyone was coughing and choking.

Carlson and I stopped at Emily's desk in the front office. It had one shotgun hole and dozens of automatic rounds.

It looked more like a giant lump of Swiss cheese than it did an office desk.

The Lieutenant took me by the arm, firmly. "Listen Diamond. You've got to prepare yourself. It's bad."

"What is it? What did they find?"

He walked me into my office. The room had been ransacked. Books and papers lay everywhere. The room had been as shot up as the front office. "I don't understand," I started to say, then stopped, seeing my desk. A sheet was draped over one end, covering some sort of bloody mess. My heart sank, not knowing what to expect. Carlson, grim and perspiring lifted the sheet so I could see.

I stared blankly, uncomprehending, at the mass of bloody tissue laying on my desk. Horrified, I suddenly realized that it was the shot up remains of two female breasts.

I reeled backward in disbelief. "My god!" I gasped. "No! Sonofabitch, my God, no!" I backed right into the wall- what was left of it. "What kind of monster could do that...to an innocent..." Then: "What could I have possibly done to cause something like this?"

Carlson shook his head, putting his hand on my shoulder. "Whoever did this; and for whatever reason, you didn't cause it. This is madness, and we'll find out who is responsible."

My teeth were clenched, but my whole body was shaking. "I better not find them first! Lieu, I want to talk to the two gorillas. They must know something."

He looked at me for a moment. "I know interviews were your strong suit, Diamond. I'll have to think about it. Actually, I think you have a passion that might produce some results...but I can't have you going off on them."

"Have they lawyered up?"

"No, they won't say anything. Other than repeat the names that are on their driver's licenses. We know that's crap from their prints."

"Let's go," I said. "I have to get out of here."

The Talking Dog Says

He nodded, sympathetic. Over his shoulder he called to one of the detectives. "I want everything you have on this, the minute you have it."

My thoughts and feelings were flying in every direction. I was filled with grief and guilt about Emily. If she was still living, she was in an unfathomable amount of pain, and without medical attention, wouldn't survive very long. It might have helped if I had some idea why this was happening. I hadn't been to New York in several years, and I had joked about Chicago, but I hadn't been in that windy town for close to a decade. How the hell could I have pissed off the Jersey mob enough to initiate such retaliation?

There were enough missing puzzle pieces that the whole picture was un-recognizable. The frustration, along with the sorrow and pain was overwhelming me. Carlson made conversation as we drove back to the 5th Avenue station. I didn't hear a word of it, lost in thought. Then I did hear him chuckle. I looked at him, a bit annoyed to have my troubles interrupted by mirth.

"Don't worry. We're going to get to the bottom of all this." The man was a mind reader now too. "There's a ton of forensic evidence in that office. In the end, we'll know more about them then they know about themselves."

I nodded. "If it's Mob connected, we might not ever find out who ordered or carried it out. We might never find out *why!*"

"We'll find out," he assured me. "This may just be Minneapolis, but I have a few friends and connections out East. Even the Mob can be negotiated with- you just have to know who to talk to, and what to say."

I walked back into the station like a zombie. My legs felt weak. Several times I had to balance myself by touching the wall. Carlson told me to sit tight while he checked on the progress being made with the two would-be assassins. As I waited, I realized what I had to do. I had to call G.H.

G.H. was an old friend. He'd been big in the CIA decades earlier. Now retired from all that, he still kept up with his Intelligence buddies, and loved getting back into the business for short excursions. What he didn't know, he could find out fast, if need be.

I sat down, flipped open my cellphone.

"Hello?"

"Herbie, it's Jim Diamond."

"Well hello Diamond. Been a long time. How is it up there in the frozen tundra?"

"I need your help. It's urgent."

His tone instantly switched away from light-heartedness to business. "What's going on, Jim?"

"Frankly sir, I don't know. Two goons tried to waste me in my house last night, and this morning my office was destroyed, and my secretary…Sir, they mutilated my secretary and left her flesh on my desk."

"Good Lord, Jim!"

"Yeah…She's missing. We're pretty certain she's dead."

"That's horrible. I'm so sorry. What can I do?" That was G.H. : a very caring, giving CIA hard guy.

"We've got the two assailants from last night. Big time perps with Jersey mob affiliations. A 'Jack Bickford', and a 'Harry Carter.' Do you think you could check up on them for me…We've got their Jackets, but nothing that tells us why they're after me."

"Where are you now, Jim?"

"I'm with Minneapolis Homicide. The Lieutenant might let me take a run at the two Goons: they've clammed up. The police think my present state of mind could be helpful. You know I can work an interview."

"Be careful. This is cruel and awful stuff. I'll make some calls, and get back to you. You on your cellphone?"

"Yes Herbie. Thanks."

"Oh, and Jim."

"Sir?"

"Don't go too far in that Interview room. You're very upset- don't go overboard and get those two sprung on technicalities."

"Thanks Herbie. I won't."

Carlson had walked up to me. "Can I ask who you were talking to about this situation, Mr. Diamond?"

"Nothing to worry about." I told him it was Gerald Markinson.

"He can't do anything."

"Yes sir, but he has connections. I'll get the inside scoop that a Jacket doesn't give us. It can't hurt…I've used him before, but only when the going gets rough. I mean no offense to you or your detectives. It's just another avenue to explore. Could be useful. He just expects discretion, Lieutenant."

He rubbed his forehead with one hand. "Alright; but I would have appreciated a heads-up, and will expect one in the future. I don't need any interference no matter how high it comes from."

"He won't get in your way. He's just helping me out. He likes me…"

"Well, there's no accounting for taste, Diamond. Do you want to have a formal introduction to your so-called burglars now?"

"Yes. Tell me, has Emily's mother been informed of the situation? She lives on Snelling."

"Someone's on the way over there."

The Interview rooms were on the other end of the Homicide division, away from Carlson's office. As we walked, the Lieutenant filled me in. "We're going to talk to Bickford first. He's a total scumbag, but not a cold blooded murderer like his assassin friend, Carter." He took ahold of my arm. "Now look. Your participation can be revoked in an instant, Diamond. You do anything that makes me regret your presence, and I swear to God, you'll be regretting it too. Your participation in the Carter interview depends on how well this goes."

I nodded. "I won't touch him Lieu. Promise." But I went in snarling. "So you're the dirty piece of dog shit that tried to kill me yesterday. Not to mention blowing up my office and killing my goddam secretary this morning." I leaned down, in his face.

He looked up at me, frowning, not totally unaffected by my cute entrance. His nose was stitched like it was cloned from Frankenstein's monster, twice the size it had been before the introduction to my wine bottle. His upper lip had been cut and stitched too, and now, sneering at me, he looked as ugly as any sonofabitch I'd ever laid eyes upon.

I grunted a laugh. "Ever seen a puss like that, Lieu?"

Carlson said nothing.

"Listen asshole," I continued. I don't mind a little tussle between friends, but I was pretty fond of that secretary of mine, and I'm afraid you've bitten off more than you can handle, getting in between Mafia killers and *my* pissed off sorry ass!"

"I don't know nothing about no secretary."

"Right. It's just a coincidence that you tried to whack me last night, and my whole world was blown to bits this morning." I looked at Carlson. "Can you believe this garbage? First thing this stupid bastard can think to say, and it's pure crap.

"Bickford, we've already talked to Carter. Sad to say, I broke every tooth in the front of his mouth." I got close again. "Kind of looks like Carlsbad Caverns when he opens his mouth…Anyway, whether it was pain or humiliation, he's talking. Oh, I take that back- he's writing notes. He won't be talking for a good long time." I feigned a laugh. "Or eating…or smiling…"

"He wouldn't say nothing."

"He says he was along for the ride: that you offered him some major cash to help him out on this."

The Talking Dog Says

"He didn't say nothing!"

"He said that you were a moron, and screwed up the whole deal, but all right. Have it your way, dumbass. We don't much care about either of you, and if we can get one of you, we're going to go for it. This case is sure to go Federal, Bickford. By the time Carter gets done talking you could be up for an injection."

"He..." he started, but then said nothing.

"Come on Lieu." I moved toward the door. "Let's get out of here. I'm going to enjoy seeing this asshole die for killing my Emmie."

Carlson followed me out. I walked back toward his office, but stopped at a bench in the hall, collapsing wearily. "That was...draining."

He sat down beside me. "Not a bad interview. It could work."

"Thanks."

"How come you quit? You would have made a good Detective."

I shrugged. "Just too routine. I was drowning in red tape and bullshit."

"It's a shame. You..."

He didn't get to finish the compliment. My cellphone rang.

I stood up. "That'll be G.H."

"Take it. We'll interview Carter when you're done."

It was G.H. He never wasted any time. "Jim, you were going in the wrong direction...Yes, it's true, Carter has likely performed as many as a half dozen hits in his time, but he's washed up, for the most part...He had a stroke two years ago, and never really fully recovered. He's doing what he can find...Lately, he's been doing some "security" work for an Armand Backus in Las Vegas. Nothing illegal so far, unless invasion and mutilation is Mr. Backus's idea of security."

"Vegas? I haven't been in Vegas since last summer. And I've never met any Armand Backus."

"He's more or less a loan shark with some financial holdings. He used to be an entertainer, singing under some other name, but that all went down the tubes. The FBI is investigating him on several fronts. Apparently, he's also... how should I say this...He's 'light in the loafers.'"

Light in the loafers? I almost laughed, but stifled it. "He's gay."

"Apparently, but stuck in the closet big time."

"Herbie, you sure find out everything."

"He's also, apparently, a very enthusiastic Elvis Presley fan. Loves everything about him- collects Presley memorabilia. Imagines he's following in the 'King's footsteps...might be a way to get at him."

"Find some way to adore Elvis too?"

"Shouldn't be too hard for you, Jimmy. I always imagined you to be a bit of a modster. A real cool cat." I could hear him snickering in the background.

"I'll try to think of something, Herbie. Thanks for the vote of confidence."

"Listen Jim; the FBI is interested in talking to you. They want to get Backus. One of their guys got run off the road and killed while investigating him. They know he did it: they just don't have anything to prove it. Backus is always covered when his dirty work goes down. He uses guys like Carter and Bickford and he pays them well to take the fall if they have to."

"And his money is coming from criminal activities?" I asked.

"Oh, he has some money left from his singing days, but yes, they think he's behind a lot of illegal activity down there.

"Jim, I know you. You likely have one foot already out the door headed for Las Vegas...I want you to meet up with the Agent heading up those investigations. FBI: An old friend of mine named Keyes. They want to talk to you, and

The Talking Dog Says

I'm betting they can help you just as much as you can help them."

"I'll sure do that, sir. I can't tell you how much I appreciate the help."

"Glad to help. The Missus and I are just sick about your secretary- Such a horrid, inhuman thing to do. We want to see those sickos brought to justice, but Jim, you be careful out there. This Backus fellow is no one to mess with, especially if you succeed in tying him to your office and secretary. He'll want to shut you up."

I'll be careful, sir. Thanks again for everything."

I hung up the phone, turned. Carlson was waiting for me across the room.

"Anything?"

I had to tell him if I wanted to use any of this information to go at Carter. I filled him in on what I'd been told.

He nodded when I finished. "Should come in handy. Shall we go take down our assassin?"

I followed him back into the hall, three rooms down from where we'd spoken to Bickford. It occurred to me that Carlson seemed to be enjoying my company. I'm guessing in normal circumstances, he left this sort of thing to his detectives, and didn't mind the change in routine. We found Carter sitting at the interview room table. He gave us each a sneer as we walked in. He was a bigger man than his accomplice, more imposing. His jaw was swollen, but not broken, as I'd told Bickford. He wasn't missing any teeth, but his chin did have a nasty gash in it. He looked, I must say, just like central casting had sent over their best beat-up thug.

Carlson started it off. "This is going to be short, Carter. Your buddy is a regular songbird, you know that?"

He didn't move or say a word. Probably thought we were lying, that we didn't know anything. I helped him along: "Carter, we know you're working for Backus. We know he sent you here to kill me. And we can tie you to the assholes we caught today destroying my office. They killed my secretary. You are going to Federal court on this one, and then to Death Row."

His façade melted, but only for a moment. "You don't know shit. I don't know any Backus."

"We know he sent you here to do his dirty work while he's safely back in Vegas seducing young men.... Tell me something, Carter. Do you do that for him too?" Carlson wasn't so bad at this either.

"I ain't no fruit."

"Well that's lovely, Harry. But you are a murdering scumbag and we've got you this time." Carlson spoke quietly, real matter of fact. He leaned into Carter, like I'd leaned on the other rat, but with a completely different attitude. "We've got the DA with Mr. Bickford at this very moment. He's cutting a sweet deal too...You see we believe him when he says he just was hired to go with you...You really aren't the same dependable killer since your stroke. Are you Harry? You need help, and unfortunately for you and your elegant boss, you picked someone who couldn't wait to sing and cut a deal."

I really admired his approach. It was almost the exact opposite of how I'd handled Bickford, but it was the right way. Harry Carter didn't flinch or sag in his chair, or show any defeat, but he did start moving both legs up and down rapidly, anxiously. He wasn't bright enough to hide that little tic.

"Well," continued the Lieutenant. "That's about all we have to say. We're going to book you for attempted murder on Mr. Diamond here, and also conspiracy to commit murder in regards to his secretary." He moved toward the door. "Diamond, I think we're done here."

"Someone will be in to book you shortly," I added. "If they don't end up giving you an injection I'll see you again in twenty, maybe thirty years."

"Wait!" he blurted out. We both stopped and faced him.

The Talking Dog Says

"What if I was to give you information too?"

"What kind of information?" Carlson asked.

"Backus. About Backus."

"We'd be interested to hear what you have to say... but don't expect miracles. You're in a mess here, and your buddy has already told us a lot."

"Yeah, well I know some big stuff. Might just make roughing up this little pussy seem like small potatoes..." I almost laughed at that. "And I don't know nothing bout no conspiracy to kill no secretary...Can you get a DA to talk with me too?" He was feeling sure of himself, thinking that dangling unknown secrets in front of us would make us curious. He was leaning back in his chair so the front legs came up off the floor. Classic cocky a-hole behavior that demanded a classic police response.

"I'll see if they have time for you," Carlson smiled, passing him, to the door. I followed, knocking my foot against the back leg of his chair. 'Mr. Smug As a Bug' fell like a sack of cement, twisting because of the one arm cuffed to the table. He hit the floor with a thud, and surprisingly was back on his feet in seconds.

"Sorry," I smiled. "I tripped."

"Lousy bastard," he said, menacingly, through clenched teeth. "You wouldn't get away with that if I was free."

"Harry, you aren't ever going to be free again." Carlson and I walked out of the room. I was grinning.

"Diamond, I told you..."

"Didn't promise you nothing this time, Lieu."

"I expected your promise to last the day," he said, disapproving. I could tell, however, that he really wasn't angry. Carter would have no telltale marks, and anyway, I tripped on the chair leg jutting up and away from the floor.

"I think the DA is going to be pretty happy with you Lieutenant. You're handing them some big stuff here...Anyway, I wanted to wipe some of that smugness away. If he's as big a killer as I think he is, he could have dropped into Hell for all I care."

"What I want to know," he said, abruptly, grabbing me once again by the arm to keep me in place. "Is are you going to stand down and let us handle this. It appears that we're about to uncover a treasure chest of information that will get this Backus indicted. I don't really like the thought of you going down there and mucking it up."

"Yeah, actually Lieu, I think it is best I lay low."

"I can give you some protection."

I shook my head. "Naw. I'm a big boy. My gun won't be on the other side of the room from here on in."

"Alright then. If you change your mind you call. Until we get this thing in hand I'll be worrying about your stupid ass!"

I grinned. "Thanks...You know, thish could be the beginning of a beautiful friendship." My best Bogart impersonation.

"Get the hell out of here," he snapped, and I did.

He insisted on sending me home in a patrol car. My place turned out to be quiet, and not newly molested. I waved goodbye to the officer. I almost felt guilty, bald faced lying to a guy who had shown me more caring in these few hours, than he had the entire rest of our relationship. I'd get over it.

I had to walk around the house and let myself in the back door- the front door still needing a professional fix. Safely inside, I grabbed a beer from the refrigerator, and sat in the recliner to call a friend- Chet Hardy. Chet owned his own Cessna. A businessman, retired wealthy, and now just a flying playboy, I retained him as my personal pilot when times were good for me, and he just flew me around when times weren't so good.

I had long ago tired of commercial airlines. These days the terrorists can get on the plane and go wherever they want with explosives and weapons up their Hole, or strapped to their privates. But, if you're a three-year-old

The Talking Dog Says

American born boy with the same name as some dickhead on the No Fly List, then you aren't going anywhere. The whole Security measure system is just a crock of shit to make us think we're safe.

Chet was up for some time in Las Vegas and told me he could be fueled up and ready to go in five hours. "It can wait til morning," I said. I still had to book a hotel room, which in Vegas shouldn't be too hard, even at the last minute. And I really didn't see the sense of arriving in the middle of the night. I also needed to reach Kathleen so she would know I had to leave town for awhile.

Unfortunately, I didn't have any idea how to go about it. If they had her in a Safe House, no one would be giving me her number, brother or not. I sat down in my recliner, watching some mindless television, thinking about her. Just after supper, my cell phone rang, and it was Kathleen.

"How are you doing?"

"I'm okay, Jim. Just don't ask where I am."

"Did you know Steve is in jail?"

A pause. "No. Really! What did he do now?"

"They locked him up for what he did to you honey. They're throwing away the key for as long as they can get away with it."

"He isn't going to like that."

"Too damn bad," I said. "None of that matters now, Kathy. You're safe, and we're going to keep you safe."

"I can't stay in here forever."

"No. Hopefully Steve will find someone new and move on. Even so, it might be a good idea if you moved to a new place."

"Yes Jim. I don't want to go back to that apartment."

"I'll take care of it, honey. Listen, I have to go out of town for a week or so. There was some trouble at my office. I have to look into some things. Are you going to be okay?"

"Sure. I've got lots of support here. I'm not going anywhere any time soon. What happened, Jim? Does it have anything to do with Steve?"

"No. Nothing. He's innocent on this one. Just some detective work…You know it never ends."

"Alright. Jim, I have to go. I'm only allowed ten minutes of phone calls a day, and I need to talk to mom."

"Call me anytime, Kathy. I won't be so busy that I can't speak with you."

Chet was waiting for me the next morning at the Eden Prairie Airport- Flying Cloud. Chet always had a wide grin, but it was even broader and merrier today. He was only hours away from the hookers. If he was a fair example of playboy pilots, they do enjoy their hookers.

I loaded my bags into the airplane hold, my gun stowed away safely. My license didn't cover Las Vegas, but a Shamus without a gun is like a preacher without a bible. There was solid reason to believe I would need it on this trip. I'd have to worry about any consequences later.

I met Emily Blake after I started dating her mother, Marian. She was a bright-eyed, newly graduated high schooler, headed for college. On semester breaks, she started doing some office work for a very disorganized private eye. When summer came, she spent it creating a filing system that had been sorely needed by The Diamond Agency. Then she graduated, a degree in Economics hanging on her living room wall, but somehow never left my employ, even though her mother and I drifted apart.

Through the years, we'd come to a close father-daughter relationship, and nothing else. The wasting of her education, however, didn't sit well with her mother. In Marian's mind, I might as well be a moral deficient. I was preventing Emily from pursuing the life of a rich and famous economist, and not just that, throwing away her hard work in school to file papers and empty waste baskets.

The Talking Dog Says

Emmie had never known her father, and it bothered her. She compensated by adopting me, and transforming my office into a masterful, organized, professional place of business. We joked that she knew what I needed before I often did, right down to bringing me coffee as I stood up to go make it myself. My case materials were always in impeccable order, as was everything else I needed throughout the day.

The hate and rage that I felt in my heart for those who were responsible for taking her away from me, was almost more than I could bear. Her mother must be going through Hell, but I couldn't bring myself to call Marian. *Her* hate and rage was a gigantic guilt trip I didn't need right now. I was shouldering the blame enough all on my own.

I stared out the window of the Cessna nearly the entire flight. Chet noticed my sullen mood, calling me over the intercom. "What's going on, buddy? I've never seen someone go to Las Vegas looking so depressed!"

I got out of my chair and stood in the cockpit doorway. I filled Chet in.

"Sons of bitches," he said, shaking his head. "That Backus sounds crazy. He could have some dangerous people around him. You need help, Jim?"

"I might, but he sent two absolute idiots to my house."

"Yeah, but then he destroyed your office, and killed your secretary."

He had a point.

"The FBI is investigating Backus already. They want to meet with me. The guy in charge is a friend of G.H.'s."

"Well then," he said- the big grin was back. "I won't worry about you while I'm cavorting with the show girls."

I laughed. The only show girls Chet ever hooked up with were the kind who only put on private performances. "I wouldn't want that on my conscience, Chet!"

We arrived at McCarran just after Noon. It was fiercely hot out on the runaway, a bit unusual for this early in the year. The air conditioned terminal was a great relief. I was perspiring by the time I got to the baggage claim area to look for my bags. There was, of course, a delay. I spent some time dropping coins in a very conveniently placed slot machine. I expected to lose every cent, and I wasn't disappointed. What happens in Vegas, stays in Vegas, including my money.

The bags finally arrived, and I headed out the door to find a taxi. I had decided not to rent a car, at least not immediately. Cabs are plentiful, and in most cases, the drivers know the area much better than the tourist.

G.H. had told me that Agent Keyes would find me once I arrived. I hadn't spotted anyone at the airport, but he and a buddy were waiting for me at the Mirage. I saw them, off to the side, trying not to be noticed, and watch me at the same time. They both looked a thousand percent like FBI. One of them had a plug in his ear: he couldn't be more obvious to anyone with half an ounce of brains; which, by the way, isn't required in Las Vegas. God help the economy of the town if it ever is demanded.

Neither man moved a muscle, staying where they were while I checked in. I assumed they'd follow me into the elevator, and make contact there, but neither did. The elevator door closed, and I ascended with only the usual bellhop banter about enjoying my stay for company.

The bellhop opened my room presented it to me as though I were walking into a palace. It took about a minute for him to give his spiel, collect his tip, and leave. I desperately wanted a shower, a nap, and a drink, not necessarily in that order. Any hope of getting them was dashed when the telephone in the room began ringing.

"Hello?"

"Mr. Diamond. It's Agent Keyes." It was a woman's voice. "I've arranged for a private conference room in the

The Talking Dog Says

Mirage so we can speak to you. I'm sorry to bother you so soon, but would you mind meeting with us right away?"

"Sure. I'll be right down." I sighed, tucking my suitcases into a bureau drawer. The gun should be safe there. I shoved the room pass card in my pocket and headed downstairs, wondering who the two men in the hotel lobby were, half expecting I'd find them in the same spot I'd seen them. Instead, there was only the hotel concierge.

"Mr. Diamond? Right this way, sir." I followed him into an employees only hallway, mostly obscured from sight by a large tropical plant. I was ushered into a small conference room where a woman and a man were waiting. "Who...?"

The woman stepped forward. "I'm Agent Amanda Keyes. I believe our mutual friend gave you my name." She motioned to the man. "My partner, Agent Ken Burley. We'd like to talk to you about the attempt on your life, and the attack on your office."

"And the murder of my secretary...Hey look, I have a question before we get started. Do you have other Agents in this hotel?"

"No," said Keyes. "What's this about?"

"When I checked in there were two other men in the lobby watching. They had to be Agents. I figured one of them was you, Keyes. G.H. didn't mention you were a woman."

She smiled slightly. "We don't have anyone else here today. Did you notice them, Ken?"

Burley shook his head.

I didn't know if they were telling me the truth, or not; but didn't know why they would lie. And, if they didn't see something so obvious, my confidence didn't exactly soar. Of course, the two could have left the second I came upstairs. "At least one of them had a plug in his ear. Seemed rather obvious, though I was expecting you to be waiting for me."

"Could have been hotel security, or something local," Burley offered. "I'll check on that."

Keyes nodded; moving on. "I have a couple of reports from the Minneapolis police. We are sorry about your secretary: absolutely appalling. I spoke briefly with a Lieutenant Carlson, Mr. Diamond. He was rather surprised to hear you were headed out here, and that I was meeting with you."

"I lied to him. I said I'd lay low while he investigated."

"Well, our mutual friend knows you better. He told me you'd be out here right away."

"Carlson and I don't get along too well. I just couldn't sit still after my office was destroyed. The girl was like a daughter to me. When our friend found out that Backus was likely behind the whole thing it was a no-brainer. Sharing it with the Minneapolis police would have caused problems."

"Well, we are glad you're here. It does save us some time, but I will insist that you be a little more forthright with us."

"Understood. I'll do everything I can to help."

"Now, Mr. Diamond: I understand you were in Las Vegas last summer?"

"Yes."

"Were you working?"

"No. Rest and relaxation."

"Did Miss Blake come with you?"

"No. I came alone. I met some girls here."

"Did you see or meet Armand Backus on that trip, or any time before that?"

"Never. I have found out that he was a singer named..."

"Jackie Midnight," Burley said.

"Yeah, Midnight. He had a song about a Talking Dog, or something like that. Stupidest damned song I've ever been subjected to."

"But you never met him?"

The Talking Dog Says

"Neither as Midnight or Backus...I'd long ago forgotten the singer, and I never heard his real name until G.H. gave it to me."

"Who did you see down here?" Burley asked.

I shrugged. "I met a couple girls. Hung around with one in particular; her name escapes me...Melissa, I think. No. Melinda. Nice girl, a lot of fun."

The two Agents looked at each other. "Do you remember her last name, Mr. Diamond?"

"I don't know if I ever knew it."

A briefcase was sitting on the table in front of Keyes. She opened it, shuffling through some papers, then withdrew a photograph. and slid it across the table to me.

"Christ," I exclaimed. "That's her! Who the hell is she?"

"Backus's girlfriend," said Burley. "Melinda Rae Menendez."

"Girlfriend? I was told..."

"That Armand Backus is gay? He is."

I didn't ask him how he knew that, but it probably involved pictures, videos, and hidden microphones.

"She's a beard," Keyes said. "She makes him look straight, and the whole gay thing seems like an ugly rumor."

"I didn't know. She didn't mention him, or any boyfriend at all. We had a great time. I didn't sense she was cheating, or trying to hide it."

"Literally, she probably wasn't cheating. Only contractually: Backus probably paid her a whole lot of money for a convincing girlfriend act."

I saw a little bit of light. "That's why he targeted me? He knows I was with her last summer?"

"Might be: looks that way," Keyes agreed.

"Maybe I can get near her again...see what she knows about him?"

"Well, that's a problem, Mr. Diamond. We can't speak with her. Melinda Menendez went missing just after you were down here. She hasn't been seen in almost ten months.

"Ten months!"

"Yes," Burley said, leaning forward. "You were one of the last people she was with before she disappeared.

Oh Shit. Could this be taking an uglier turn?

Burley continued, an unlikeable gleam in his eyes. "I would imagine that killing Backus's girlfriend might also explain his rage, not to mention the horrible act against your secretary, daughter, friend."

He was being a big Puke. I gave him a second look to determine his age. Arlo Guthrie famously said that you never become a full FBI Agent until you've had twenty five years with the department, because it takes that long to learn to be that big a bastard. He didn't look old enough, but he did meet the qualification.

"Kiss my ass, Agent Burley...You seriously think I had something to do with her disappearance? That girl and I had a lot of fun together. I left her with fond memories, but I didn't much know or care who, if anyone, she belonged to."

Keyes patted the air with both hands. "Agent Burley apologizes for his impetuousness, Mr. Diamond. You understand that we have to examine every angle. Your time with that girl does provide a motive for her disappearance and probable murder, but if it makes you feel any better, I don't think you had anything to do with it. We just have to ask the questions."

"Insinuating such a thing is not appreciated."

"Understood, Mr. Diamond. We have to ask...As long as this minor unpleasantness has come up, I want to remind you that you are here at our leave. Anytime it is decided that you are a problem or hindrance you will be on a plane back to Minneapolis."

"Coach and at your own expense," added Burley.

"Yes ma'am," I said. What else could I say?

"So let's keep the personal animosities to ourselves." She looked in Burley's direction too. "Mr. Diamond, what

The Talking Dog Says

would you think about making your story public? Planting it in the media."

"Telling them what, exactly?"

"We'd like to announce a new investigation of Armand Backus regarding the disappearance of Melinda Menendez, and what happened to you. An investigation based on the testimony from a Minneapolis witness."

"You want to shake him up?"

"Yes, and what will shake him up most is that the story is literally true," Burley observed. "However, we'd like to suggest that the girl told you things that implicate him in all of his shady dealings, as well as her disappearance, and the attacks on you."

I smiled. "If that doesn't rattle his cage, I could contact him, and ask for hush money."

"To make a deal for your silence? You know this guy plays rough."

"No one has to tell me that," I reminded them. "Shotguns and machine guns, and severed body parts. The police are likely still doing forensics on my office."

Keyes was thinking. "That'll work as long as the payoffs are his idea. Are you willing to wear a wire?"

I nodded. "As long as we're somewhere we can control. I don't want to end up shot full of holes, big or small; or be missing valuable body attachments. I don't want to be desert soil fertilizer either, which is probably where we'll find Melinda Menendez."

"We'll insist on public places, and be close by, Mr. Diamond."

"Alright. Let's do it."

Keyes was frowning. "I'm troubled by your story about those two men. I'd like to also put a couple Agents on this floor to keep an eye on anyone coming and going. Those two mystery men could be Backus's advance scouts. Tell me, what did they look like?"

"The first one is tall. Six three, maybe. Six four. He was thin and gaunt. Looked like he doesn't eat much. The other guy was much shorter. He had longer hair, touching his shoulders. Big teeth and glasses- he kind of looked like a gopher. A real odd couple."

"Did you see any weapons?"

"No...I don't mind the guard. Just keep them out of my way. I want to be able to act like a normal tourist.

"How long will it take to get the news story out?"

"It'll be on the evening news."

Pretty quick.

"Ken, notify Agents Marks and Agent Simpson to get down here and take the first watch."

"Before you go," I asked. "Can you tell me what other things you're working on with Backus. I want to know as well as possible what I'm dealing with."

Keyes smiled, ever so faintly. "It's all in the newspapers. That'll give you something to do while you're waiting. Seriously, Mr. Diamond. You know that he probably conspired to have you killed, shot up your office and likely murdered your secretary in a barbaric and horrible way. Sir, what more could I possibly say that could make you appreciate the situation more than you already do?"

She was right, but I resolved to visit the Las Vegas Sun anyway. "I'll check out the newspapers. Every bit of information helps me know how to handle this sick bastard."

"Just don't get ahead of the program, Diamond. You lie to me like you lied to Minneapolis Homicide and we will ship you back to Minneapolis without a couple body parts."

I smiled. "Yes. You're in charge, Agent Keyes."

"Good. Thank you for your cooperation." As they left the conference room, Agent Burley was smirking.

The evening news did a thorough job. Whoever Keyes had for a contact, the story was written and on the air in less than two hours. The local stations built their entire show around the various aspects of Armand Backus's former celebrity, legal troubles, and now, allegations of intrigue and murder. The major networks reported the new development, they even had my name, and pictures of my office building and Melinda Menendez and Emily Blake. Emmie's mother would never forgive me for that, but it did put faces on the investigation which would affect public opinion.

The cable news networks went on a feeding frenzy, as they always do when something happens, doesn't happen, or is about to happen or not happen. Each network had a team planted outside of the Mercury Hotel where Armand Backus lived, in a normally more quiet, private part of Las Vegas. Each had some drone whining on endless suppositions and hypotheses along with the basic facts, until they had damn near invented an entirely different story.

I also got more than my fill of Backus—Jackie Midnight's stupid dog song: *'The Talking Dog says Bow. The talking Dog says Wow...'* Over a million people had bought that horrid piece of shit song. Even as a novelty it was pretty pathetic. I turned the television off. I wanted to throw him in prison for that crime alone.

I was tired, yawning; and decided to take a nap. I laid down on the bed, stretching, and then, predictably, my cell phone rang. I reached over to the nightstand, unplugging it from the charger, checking the caller information. 'Minneapolis Police.' Lieutenant Victor Carlson, no doubt, calling to offer his support and good will. I let it go to voice mail. No message.

I plugged the phone back into the charger, then laid back down for my nap. I'd been asleep about a half hour when the hotel telephone began ringing. Damned Carlson, I thought. Persistent.

Sitting up, I grabbed for the telephone, which had rung a half dozen times by the time I got to it, having decided I'd better answer it."

"Hello."

"Mr. Diamond, I do hope I have not awakened you?" Manners: it sure as hell wasn't Victor Carlson.

"Sort of. Who is this?"

"This is Armand Backus." That didn't take long. He continued, "Mr. Diamond, I wonder if we might get together. I'd like to straighten out these wild misconceptions you might have about me."

"I'd like that, sir. I have to warn you though. I have frigging FBI bastards checking on me. *They* seem to have those misconceptions, and they're leaning on me quite heavily to support their accusations."

"Really! I was under the impression from this evenings news that you flew down here to accuse me of all manner of wrongdoing."

I couldn't believe the gall of this guy, though I had to admit, I never heard a more literate liar this far from D.C., in all my life. "Mr. Backus, you must understand: those reports were planted by the Bureau. You've got me all wrong."

"How intriguing."

"I'm actually quite a fan of your singing career. I've got all of your records, and several on compact disc. I never dreamed I'd ever meet you."

"Though you think I've had something to do with trying to harm you?"

"Quite frankly, I don't know what to think. As I said, the FBI is pressuring me to make some public statements. Those news stories were meant to ratchet up the pressure. I rather resent how I'm being treated."

It was exactly the right thing to say. "Well," he said. "We surely must meet, Mr. Diamond. When might you have some time for me?"

"Sometime tomorrow. They're following me every time I leave the building. I'll have to go through the kitchen to get out...Is there somewhere private we could bump into each other?"

"Yes. An exclusive club in the Cooper Building. It's the Radar Syncopation Club. I'll leave your name with the Security desk. We can have a drink without anyone bothering us."

"After lunch?" I suggested. "Say one o'clock."

"One will be fine."

"I look forward to meeting you. I've been a fan of yours forever." I'd already said that, but I'm sure his ego didn't mind it being repeated.

"Thank you, Mr. Diamond. Until then..."

I didn't expect him to fall hook, line, and sinker for my compliments, but I could tell it had touched his egomaniacal nature. I never met a washed up performer who didn't eat up flattery with a tablespoon, and I had more sugar to dish out too.

Switching to my cell phone, I found Chet's number. I needed to reach him before the women came out to roost. He sounded only a little lit up. "Speak to me!"

"Hey Buddy, it's Jim. Can you talk?"

"Yeah. I'm in a bar downtown. I'm coming up to the Strip in a bit." *For a Hooker, no doubt.* "What's up, Jim? You don't sound like you're having any fun."

"Did you see the evening news."

He laughed. "Next question."

"Well, the FBI is going public with my presence here. I just had a conversation with our Bad Guy. He's invited me to cocktails tomorrow. I need to meet you in the morning at a high end gift shop."

"Just how early?"

I laughed again. "Eleven will do, but I need you to get some stuff off of the airplane, so you can slip it to me at this meet."

"Why this gift shop?"

"I have to pick up something for my new friend. Something I can put the flat device into- probably some kind of ink pen. This guy likes Elvis so I'm going to tell him it was once owned by the King."

Chet laughed. "Just make sure you get rid of the receipt before you give it to him, Jim."

I chuckled. "Bring the recorder too: the whole briefcase. And Chet, I'm booking a room at the Mercury Hotel where Backus stays. I'll let you know the room number."

"Sounds like I better party while I can."

"Not too much partying, Chet. I'm only going to have this one opportunity to do this."

"No problem: Into the girlies, Jim. Not the booze."

Another liar, but I let it pass. "I'll meet you at Maloy's in the Beazley Mall, at eleven sharp, Chet."

"You got it. Hey, I'm coming up to Caesar's. Are you sure you don't want to have a couple of drinks?"

"It'll have to wait, Chet. I have to let my FBI contacts know what's going on- well most of it, anyway. Being hung over tomorrow won't help me: I want to be my best going up against this lunatic."

"Alright. Alright. Wish me luck tonight."

Luck.

I went into the hallway. The two Agents were down by the ice machine, pretending they had just run into each other while fetching ice. To their credit, they looked the part. The one was wearing an oversized T-shirt and sweatpants, and the other had a robe over sweatpants. I couldn't see a weapon on either, but knew the guns were there.

Joining them, I picked up one of the cheap ice containers the hotel provided. "Any ice left?" I asked.

"Plenty of ice," one answered.

"The Bad Guy called, " I said, quietly, as the container filled with ice. "He's going to meet me in a club in the Cooper Building tomorrow morning. The Radar Club something." I picked up the ice bucket. "Well, you guys have a good night." I went back to my room and waited.

The Talking Dog Says

Agent Burley knocked on my door twenty minutes later. I was watching the History Channel, wondering what in God's name UFO's have to do with history. I shut the television off and filled him in on my conversation with Armand Backus.

"This is proceeding faster than we hoped for. He might believe all that silver tongued talk of yours, or more likely, enough of it that we can trap him; but I have to tell you, Mr. Diamond: This man is a dangerous sociopath We certainly appreciate it, but you've gotten yourself into quite a spot."

"No argument from me. You seem to be trying to talk me out of what you both talked me into earlier."

"Not at all. Now that it's going to happen, we only want to remind you of the danger you're placing yourself into. This guy can complement you, and blow your face off in the same instant."

I nodded. "I will try to avoid that, Agent Burley, and I do appreciate what you're saying, but it's the same risk as any undercover assignment- and I've been on some cases."

"You're right."

"I hope to show him that my secretary meant nothing to me. I wouldn't be the first callous asshole that cared more about his office than the people in it. Or, that cared about celebrity and money over everything else. I also plan to continue blaming the police and FBI. If it's one thing all criminals like hearing, it's trash talking the cops."

"What time are you meeting him?"

"One. I'm going to spend the morning acting like a tourist."

"We'll need to wire you up before that meeting. Will noon work for you? That should give us plenty of time to get you operational and to your meeting."

"Here?"

"Yes, we can meet you here. I'll see you then."

"Good night, Agent Burley."

- 47 -

My, if we weren't getting along splendidly. I'm sure his professionalism might have been tested if he had any idea that I was planning to plant my own wiretap on Backus so that I could know exactly what went on in that Penthouse. I turned the television back on to learn more about the aliens that live among us.

The next morning my FBI guards followed me out of the hotel without a word, and at a respectable distance, strolling nonchalantly behind. I hailed a moving cab, and jumped in. I looked out the back window. "There's an extra ten in it if you lose the cab that's picking up those other men."

The cabbie looked into his rearview mirror. "A plate of cake," he said, with the thickest Mid-eastern accent I'd ever heard. He turned the first corner, hit the accelerator.

"Downtown," I instructed. "Beazley Center...after you lose them."

He laughed, made another wild turn, then another, and soon we were going by the hotel entrance I had just exited. No sign of Keyes' men. We arrived at the Mall a few minutes later. I peeled off the bills, handing them over the seat. "That was one hell of a magic carpet ride!"

"Oh, Santana, sir. Yes, a very good joke indeed."

"If anyone asks about this trip, I want you to say that you were in a hurry, and that your customer asked you to slow down. Okay?"

"Oh, yes sir. Thank you, sir. You have been most generous. I will lie like a brand new carpet."

I laughed and went into the Mall, entering the first store I came to: a drug store. Looking around, as though I were searching for something, I bought some aspirin, and some Vitamin E. After last night, Chet might be needing them both about now. Then, I walked around aimlessly. I admired some art in a framing store. Stopping at a watch repair kiosk, I had them replace my battery. Leaving there,

The Talking Dog Says

casually- you never know if you have given the FBI the slip- I walked into Maloy's.

A salesperson came to me immediately. "Good morning, sir. Welcome to Maloy's. How are you this morning?"

"Fine, thanks. I'm looking for a gift for a friend. I'd like to see what you have in ink pens. I want something impressive, something undeniably special."

"We have a few, sir. Please come this way." She led me further into the store. I was impressed. This girl really had her manners straight for someone so young. I liked her. Pretty, graceful, and polite- and her ass did the most delightful dance when she walked. Priceless.

Stopping at a glass enclosed display, she inserted a key to open it. "We have some very special items." She picked up a pen. "This one is 24 carat gold with a silver stem. The ink is Italian, and manufactured with the strictest conditions."

"This one," she continued, replacing the first pen, and selecting another, barely pausing for a breath. "This one is a limited edition reproduction of a pen Liberace used. It's also gold, and the clip is actually made with African diamond chips. It's an absolute steal for six hundred and eighty dollars."

I stifled a laugh. I was looking at a Liberace reproduction for a gay Elvis wannabe. Somehow, it all seemed so perfect. "May I examine it?"

"Of course." She took the pen from its case, handed it to me. Carefully, I twisted the two sections apart, making sure not to lose the center piece. The damned ink cartridge looked like it was gold too. It was barrel shaped, but narrow toward the top. Just perfect for adding a CIA quality listening device.

"Do you have anything more gaudy?" I asked, winking, as I screwed the pen together.

"No sir," she smiled. "This is one of a kind gaudiness."

"Alright, I'll take it then. My friend is into music. I'm sure he'll like it."

"I'm sure you're correct. Cash or charge?"

As she was processing the sale, Chet sauntered in carrying my briefcase. He came to the counter, set the case down at my feet, and began looking at a rotating display of lithographs.

"Tell me something," I asked the girl. "How did you know I wouldn't go running out the door with this thing?"

"I didn't," she smiled. She patted her apron. "But I'm afraid I'd have had to shoot you." I think she was kidding, but the fierce look she gave me said I could be wrong about that.

"Good thing I didn't."

She gave me the charge slip and I signed it. She handed the pen over the counter. "Thank you sir. Please come..."

"Hey," piped up Chet, in his best loudmouth tourist voice. "Can you tell me about this thing here."

She sneaked me a look with elevated eyeballs. "Yes sir, right away." She moved down the counter to wait on him. I bent over and picked up the briefcase. As I left, I couldn't help looking back- almost fearful she would shoot me, but Chet had caused a good diversion, and was asking her some dumbass question about authenticity of the product. He couldn't have performed better.

Good thing. I was a little behind schedule. I hailed a cab back to the Mirage. Hurrying, I made my way through the busy lobby to the elevators. In my room, I set the 'spy' briefcase and the ink pen behind my suitcases for safekeeping. I laid the bag of aspirin and vitamins, on my bed. Keyes and Burley were due in minutes.

They both arrived at exactly Noon. "Our guys say you shook them this morning," Burley was looking at me rather intently.

I shrugged. "I had a cabbie with a heavy foot. I asked him to slow down."

"Did he?"

The Talking Dog Says

"Eventually. I had to raise my voice. He didn't seem to speak a great deal of English."

"So where did you go?"

"Beazley Center. I needed aspirin."

Burley actually picked up the bag on the bed to have a look. "And the Vitamin E?"

I grinned. "I'm hoping to impress a show girl later. The aspirins are for a big pain I have."

Keyes ignored that. "We better get you set up: We're going to put this unit on you." She held up a standard digital listening device to be worn under my clothing. "You can bet that he'll search you, find it, and then we'll get him with this." Keyes held up an ink pen.

I managed not to laugh. "The pen is a listening device?"

"Not exactly. It has a small device wrapped around the ink cartridge. It'll pick up everything the both of you say, and transmit it to a nearby receiver. We're going to record the whole thing."

Imagine that!

Keyes was reassuring. "We'll have an agent in that club, Mr. Diamond. If anything goes wrong, you'll have instant help."

"What if he's instantly shooting me?"

"Risk of undercover work, remember?" Burley said. "Don't worry. Backus isn't going to do something in public he can't get out of. We just want to make sure he doesn't overpower you and take you somewhere that he is comfortable shooting you."

"Good plan. I'll do anything to get him if that psycho killed my Emmie."

"Good." Burley had just finishing strapping the decoy set on my stomach. "Here's the pen. Just stick it in your breast pocket."

I turned the pen over and over. "Man, it's getting more like James Bond every day," I marveled, keeping up the dumb act. I pocketed the pen.

Keyes looked at his wristwatch. "You better get going, Mr. Diamond. Oh, and no one will be following you. Our man is already at the club. Good luck."

"I'll leave in a minute. I need to visit the bath room." I shut the hall door after they'd left. Grabbing the Maloy's bag and my briefcase, I sat down on the bed, quickly twisting the pen apart. From the briefcase I got the device and carefully placed it around the ink cartridge, then put it back together again.

It was essential that the pen worked properly. I wrote my name on a piece of paper several times. It was working fine. Next, I crumpled up the tissue paper, then wrapped it around the pen. Old Elvis mementos do not come in a gift box from Maloy's.

The Radar Syncopation Club turned out to be one of those rotating affairs at the top of the Cooper Building. True to his word, Backus had left my name with the Security desk. They pointed me to a private access elevator that went straight up to the Club, complete with an attendant.

This was more than I was accustomed to. My favorite drinking holes have about a dozen stools, a few tables, and a brassy waitress who has mastered the art of pretending she will give you anything to secure that good tip. "Have a pleasant evening, sir," the attendant said as we reached the top.

"Thanks." I exited, handing him a dollar.

The Maitre d' greeted me. "Armand Backus is expecting me," I told him.

He nodded. "This way, sir." I followed him to an end of the club that didn't look out on the Vegas skyline. I took a look around to see who was in this club. Gambling business men. What the hell did I expect? My escort led me into a small private area with a small bar, a single large table and

The Talking Dog Says

chairs. Sitting at the table was Armand Backus, and I knew it was him from the way he was dressed.

He stood to greet me, smiling broadly. "It is a pleasure to finally meet you, Mr. Diamond. I am most confident that we can discuss this matter candidly, and privately, and come to some agreement and understanding." My Super-villan was wearing an orange velvet suit, complete with purple tie. He had gaudy looking rings on most of his fingers, an earring decorated his right ear. Topping the costume off was a huge Elvis-like silver giant belt- the buckle shining through his open coat. He looked like a taco-induced nightmare, a cross between a professional wrestler and a Crayon explosion. I couldn't believe anyone had doubts about this guy's sexuality. I was willing to bet the farm.

Remaining seated at his side was a cute, barely legal slim young man who surveyed me with obvious annoyance and feminine disdain. As God is my witness, he looked like a carbon copy of the Hank Azaria character in the movie, 'The Bird Cage,' except much younger.

"You too, Mr. Midnight. I mean, Backus...I don't know..." I said, feigning confusion. I shook his hand enthusiastically. Then, putting a finger to my lips, I reached down and unbuttoned my shirt so that he could see the setup taped to my chest. By showing it to him, I hoped to disarm him; save him the trouble of searching for and finding it, and also build some trust.

He didn't miss a beat. "It's alright. Do call me Armie, Mr. Diamond. All my friends do...And this, Mr. Diamond, is my friend Starshine." I shook the boys hand. It was as satisfying as shaking an empty balloon. "Starshine," my new friend continued. "Would you search Mr. Diamond for a weapon."

The boy got up and told me to raise my arms. He sounded exactly like the Hank Azaria character as well, minus the Spanish accent. I raised my arms and when Starshine saw the apparatus strapped to my stomach, he turned to Backus.

"I'm sorry, sir," I said. "They made me wear it. Please don't hurt me." I hoped I didn't sound too convincing to my FBI listeners. I didn't need them busting this up before achieving my goals. "Starshine, would you remove that apparatus, and put it over by the juke box. Turn the music up nice and loud," Backus instructed.

Wordlessly, Starshine did as told, ripping the tape and a good deal of my chest hair off of my body. I could see he was absolutely seething, and probably couldn't expect much gentler treatment from him. He stomped off with the recorder, and a moment later, the music came up. Loud; and, of course, Jackie Midnight. Oh God, spare me the Talking Dog song.

Backus pushed me down into a chair. "Now, we can talk," he said in a quiet tone. "I appreciate that you showed me that mess. I'm sorry your acquaintance with me has caused you such pain and suffering. Would you like something to eat or drink."

I realized then how hungry I was. "Yes, I haven't eaten…something simple though….appetizer? And a Coke."

"Starshine, do find something for Mr. Diamond. Have Geoffrey put it on my account, please."

I took the pen from my pocket. "Before we get started, I brought you something. It's…it's a pen that once belonged to Elvis Presley. I know that you are quite a fan of the King's. I thought that you'd like to have it."

His mouth dropped open. He took the pen from the paper, looked it over. "What an incredibly generous gift, Mr. Diamond. Wherever did you find this treasure?"

"Well, I've been an Elvis fan as long as I've been a Jackie Midnight fan. I've got a room full of memorabilia and a few things he actually owned."

"Do you have anything I owned?" he asked, smiling.

"No…not yet, but I'm hopeful."

The Talking Dog Says

He laughed, but then was serious again. "Under the circumstances, Mr. Diamond, I don't quite understand this gift."

I raised a palm. "Look Mr. Backus...I'm in a weird situation here. I greatly admire you. I always have. I wanted you to know that, and to have this, because I knew it would be appreciated. I'm having a hard time believing that you conspired to have me killed, and destroyed my office. Leaving parts of my secretary on my desk was the sickest, insane thing I have every seen...I just can't believe you could be responsible. Please tell me you didn't do it."

A shudder ran through him. 'Starshine' had returned with a plate of chicken strips and the soda- and could tell he had missed something. He fetched Backus a drink of water, giving me another hateful look as he brought the glass to the table. I was intrigued by Backus' reaction- he seemed appalled, but I sure as hell wasn't going to let him off the hook.

I feigned new horror. "You did have something to do with it, didn't you?" I put my hand over my mouth. Acting.

He didn't know what to do. He wanted to deny it, but his lip was shaking, and he put both hands flat on the table so they wouldn't tremble. He opted for trying to explain himself, which in a court of law was almost as solid as an actual confession.

"Mr. Diamond, you have to understand. Your little pleasure trip down here last summer caused me a great deal of humiliation and embarrassment." This was a funny statement coming from a fellow wearing an orange velvet suit and all its accessories.

"You mean my time with the Menendez girl...Sir... Armie, I had no idea who the lady was. She didn't tell me anything about being attached."

"You must realize now, even though our relationship wasn't...romantic, her presence was very important to me. There are people in this world who will never accept people as they are. I was just trying to conform: I've been the subject of some hateful, hurtful speculation and innuendo."

I nodded. "I'm hoping you didn't have her murdered, and butcher her like you did my secretary."

He got the funniest look on his face. "You see..." He leaned close to me, eyeing the wire equipment sitting next to his jukebox, soaking up the tunes. He didn't know he was cozying up to the pen in my breast pocket. "One does not... always have total control over the people he hires. I deeply regret that you had to see such a thing, but I didn't order it, and was horrified when I heard about it. I never meant for anyone to be cut up like that...I was very angry. You had destroyed a myth I was trying very hard to cultivate here in Las Vegas. I never meant for any 'butchery' to happen, but I did wish to get even with you Mr. Diamond." Not an apology, nor any remorse for either girl, but we were getting closer to nailing him.

I decided to try some compassion. "One of your hired gorillas did it, didn't they? The two you hired to bump me off were morons, but the follow up team did their job, and more. I have to say, I expected to see you surrounded by them, rather than Sabu, the Jungle Boy here." I motioned at 'Starshine' whose countenance darkened.

"Armie, I think I've heard enough out of this asshole! How can you let him say such things?" the boy whined.

I ignored him. "As for your image: Armie, there's nothing wrong with being gay, or being perceived as gay. Just don't use women as your props, and stop wearing dreadful orange velvet outfits. For Christ's sakes man, a person sees you in that, what else is he going to think, other than it must be Halloween!

"People have been killed to protect a secret that's painfully obvious. It's not a secret to anyone. You are gay, and there isn't a thing you can do about it." Then, I put a hand to my face, again acting.

The Talking Dog Says

"Mr. Diamond, this is turning out to be a rather unpleasant visit."

"I'm sorry. It's just the truth. Be happy about who and what you are. You have accomplished more than I can ever hope to accomplish."

It was too much for poor Starshine. He sat, looking stunned. He picked up a bottle of tequila from the bar counter, with a look at me that seemed to say he would like nothing better than introducing it to my face, ala Jim Diamond style. Backus motioned for him to sit down.

"Armie!" he objected, but did as he was told.

A very large gorilla stepped into the room, waited for Backus to acknowledge him.

"Everything is alright Robert. Mr. Diamond will be leaving in a minute."

Kong nodded, and left.

"Look, I'm sorry about all this. I came here because I'm a fan. When I found out it was you that was behind the things that happened to me, I knew it was an opportunity to meet you...I thought that maybe we could work something out so I could forget what happened to my office... There was just a lot I didn't know about you."

"I am sorry I have shattered your illusions. I'd like to work it out also. I assume you're talking about a cash settlement?"

I said nothing, mindful of my FBI instructions to let him hang himself.

"How about five hundred thousand dollars, Mr. Diamond? Would that be enough to forget one's losses?"

"You are asking me to forget conspiracy to murder, and possibly murder in the first degree with the Menendez girl and my secretary."

Starshine jumped up, finally unable to contain himself. "I just can't stand him saying these awful things to you, Armie. My God!"

"We will be finished here in a few moments, my friend." Then to me. "Take it or leave it, Mr. Diamond. It's all I can give you."

"Then five hundred thousand will have to do."

"How long are you going to be in town?"

"As long as it takes, but don't keep me waiting. Those FBI jerks are going to be all over me if they find out about this agreement."

He leaned in close to me. "Well, they best not find out, Mr. Diamond."

"I've got a half million reasons to be quiet, Mr. Backus. Just how are you going to make this work?"

"You let me worry about that. I have several methods of hiding money."

Geez, this was good stuff. Keep talking Doggie boy.

"Let's exchange cell phone numbers, Mr. Diamond. I live in the South penthouse of the Mercury hotel. When the time is right, I will call you for a meeting, and we can settle our differences." He pushed a pad of paper and I wrote down my telephone number. He handed me a business card.

"And thanks again for the pen. I will cherish it as much as Elvis must surely have cherished it…I really wish things could have been different between us." I'd likely be cherishing the pen a lot more than he ever would if it produced some key evidence against him.

I saw no sign of my two FBI friends when I returned to the Mirage, but when I walked into the elevator, and turned around, Keyes and Burley were following me into the car. Keyes was telling Burley that there was no way in hell that Mohamed Ali could have beaten Rocky Marciano or Mike Tyson, let alone Joe Louis. Burley conceded Louis, but argued that Marciano was slow; that Ali would need only one good punch, much as Ken Norton had in their first fight.

The Talking Dog Says

He added that Ali would have outpointed Tyson, dancing away from any danger.

I enjoyed their cover patter though I didn't think either of them looked much like a fight fan. To their credit, they had researched their material so that it sounded like two friends jousting, and not two idiots revealing themselves by not knowing what they were talking about.

Following me at a distance, arguing the whole way, they paused to glance around in front of my door, then stepped into the room. I was carrying a plastic bag with their surveillance equipment in it, and handed it to Burley. "Hopefully, no one had to monitor this one. His music makes me rather nauseous."

Burley took the bag, but ignored the comment.

"Well?" I asked.

Keyes took a deep breath. "Well, I think you accomplished what we set out to accomplish. You do seem to have a knack for manipulation. However, we don't like surprises, Mr. Diamond. You failed to mention anything about that gift business."

I shrugged. "I just needed something to help sell the fan aspect. It was a last minute decision."

"Bullshit," said Burley, quietly, without malice. "You bought the pen this morning. You had more than enough time to tell us."

"I did buy it this morning. I bought it for my sister back in Minneapolis. I had it in my pocket- it was a last minute decision. I think it helped."

"It wasn't a bad idea," Keyes admitted. She stuck up a forefinger, jabbing it in the air. "But I told you that we would not tolerate rogue behavior. These little coincidences and last minute decisions that are part of dealing with you are unacceptable. We let the cabbie with a lead foot story ride, but now we discover that you used the time away from your surveillance today to purchase a gift you told us nothing about. Little details like this matter, Mr. Diamond."

"Yeah, I'm sorry...I bought it for my sister. She's going through a rough patch right now. That can be confirmed with..."

"I'm not going to argue with you, Diamond. As near as we can tell, your idea did no harm, but one more indiscretion and I won't bother to send you back to Minneapolis. I will have you locked up here."

Burley reached over and plucked their pen out of my pocket.

"So what do you want me to do now? He's going to be calling me when he gets the money together. I'm assuming you want to nail him for the hush money deal too?"

"Yes. It proves his guilt. What we want you to do while we're waiting is stand down. Be a tourist. See a show. Gamble." He handed me a card. "When Backus calls, you can arrange a meet, but you call me immediately."

I nodded, taking the card. "I think I can manage that."

"If you can't Diamond, you will regret it." Keyes assured me. "By the way: we have not been able to locate or identify those two men you saw. They weren't hotel security, and the locals are checking into it. I still have some concerns that those men are somehow connected to Backus, but after your visit with him, I doubt there's any danger. Now, he wants to settle with you and be done with it. Good day, Diamond. Call us if you hear anything." I watched her go. This was one tough woman.

After they left, I showered and changed my clothes. Taking their advice, I headed downstairs to the casino. As I'd already proven on this trip, I wasn't much of a gambler, but in my line of work, I'd had to pretend on more than one occasion. It can be a good way to meet a women that won't charge you. Good way to meet one that does.

The usual Vegas crowd had settled in for the day: Older men with short pants that nevertheless extended down to their knees to meet their black socks. Dress shirts with Texas ties. Oversized cowboy hats and preposterously decorated

The Talking Dog Says

boots that shouted 'Yeehaw.' Women with varying shades of blue hair, too much lipstick, sad and determined, sitting in front of a nickel slot machine for hours on end, doing their very best to fill them.

Someone, I forget who, said that Branson, Missouri was Las Vegas for Ugly People, but believe me, Las Vegas holds its own. Proving it, undeniably, I caught a glimpse of my own mug reflected off one of the marble and glass walls. I looked just as goofy as anyone else. At least I fit in.

I tried some blackjack, then some slots. Hell, I even tried the roulette wheel, which I consider fixed in any casino. Guess I've seen too many old films. There always seemed to be someone getting taken at Roulette. True to form, I broke even on cards, lost at the Wheel- and tanked on the slot machine. To make matters worse, no girls were charging or not charging.

More or less empty handed, I gave up, and entered the nearest restaurant, a family establishment. Hungry, but not feeling particularly enthused about anything on the menu, I ended up with a ham and cheese omelet with a beer. A combination I doubt Armand Backus or my mother would have approved, though the eggs were hot and the beer cold. My stomach growled with appreciation.

Finishing up the meal, I glanced at my watch. I would need to have a nap if I were going to be staying up all night. I returned to my room, removed my shoes, set my cell phone alarm for two hours, and went out like a light. Minutes later, it seemed; the alarm sounded, and I sat up in bed, groggy and disoriented. It was eight o'clock.

Ten minutes later, I was out on the street. The sun was going down, and the girls were starting to come out. Chet would be happy to be relieved from surveillance duty. I climbed into the first taxi in the queue, instructing the cabbie to stop at a coffee shop where I picked up a large coffee and a sandwich. As he drove, I put on a two-bit disguise: fake mustache, a pair of sunglasses, and a hat."

"Big costume party tonight?" he asked, as I slipped into an old beat up leather jacket.

"Yes. I'm going as a Sixties hippie."

"The coffee spoils it."

"Yes, but it'll keep me awake." I stuffed the sandwich package into the coat pocket. I had a few minutes as we drove across town, and I thought about what I was doing. Given that Agent Keyes was fed up with my personality, this whole surveillance operation was a huge and tragic mistake that could put both Chet and I into a Federal prison. It certainly was still worth the chance to me; I wanted to see Armand Backus and his band of thugs, every last one of them, punished for what they'd done to me, and to Emily. I always had G.H. to come to my rescue, but I knew that this had its limitations too. I hoped something would happen soon.

The cabbie dropped me off at a side entrance to the Mercury. The paparazzi had dwindled down to a few reporters and cameras at the front entrance, and things had returned to some semblance of calm. I bought a newspaper from a vendor, and walked into the hotel. I casually strolled across the modest lobby to the elevator as if the newspaper and coffee were my only two concerns in the world. If the Feds had anyone watching Backus, I hoped my sad excuse for a disguise would be enough to get me to our surveillance room undetected. I managed to find the right room, knocked and waited. I heard Chet come to the door, and look through the peep hole. The door opened.

Chet greeted me. "You look like a complete jackass in that costume."

"You still opened the door."

He shrugged. "You're the only complete jackass I know."

"Thanks buddy. No coffee for you...How's the set up working?"

"Loud and clear."

"What's he been saying: Anything about his meeting with me, or his legal troubles."

Chet shook his head slowly. "Mostly he's been thumping some boy toy named- you won't believe this…"

"Starshine."

"Yeah. Was he at your meeting today? What does he look like?"

"Small, thin. Feminine, but I got the idea he could slice me open without a second thought."

"If you get bored play some of the tape back."

"I think I've heard enough. Well, go and have fun. You're released. Just be back here by nine in the morning."

"This is going to cost you. I don't think I can take much more of their partying, Jim."

"Chet," I pointed out. "It's being recorded. You could have taken the headphones off until they were done."

"Now he tells me," he grumbled.

"Ah, Chet. One thing. The FBI isn't happy with me. They know I bought a gift for Backus, though they haven't put one and one together yet. They've given me an ultimatum. No more funny business. No lies. No surprises…Aw, this thing we're doing could put us both in some deep shit…I just wanted to let you have a chance to bail."

He grinned. "Man, if I had to do time for all the stuff you've gotten me into, I'd never get let out. I hope it's over soon, but I want to see this guy pay for what he's done."

Coffee doesn't keep you awake so much as it gives you the jitters until you fall asleep. I managed to stay awake several hours, but awakened with a start at a few minutes before three a.m. The headphones had slipped to the back of my head. I adjusted them over my ears again. I reached for what was left of my coffee.

At first, the voices were indistinct, speaking so far away from the pen that I couldn't understand much of anything. After a few minutes the people talking began to come into range so that I could hear them better. I nearly dropped my cup. I was hearing a woman's voice. There was a woman in Armand Backus's penthouse in the middle of the night. I fiddled with the receiver knobs, trying to enhance the sound. I still couldn't hear much of what was being said, but whoever it was, she sounded tired and stressed. It could be a mother or sister, I reasoned. Or was he auditioning a new beard? Could it possibly be the Menendez girl?

Abruptly, I heard a strange scraping noise, and then I couldn't hear the woman speaking anymore. A moment later, Armand Backus and his little buddy came into range, and I could hear them clearly now.

"Armie, this is all so distressing. I'm so worried about you."

"It's going to be alright. I told you: that Diamond fellow is going to be working for me. He will be selling my innocence and I intend to make him work for every cent I give to him."

"He's not FBI! They aren't going to listen to him." I was beginning to think that Starshine was the smarter of the two.

"They really don't have that much evidence, my friend. I've taken care of the two in Minneapolis. They won't be saying a damn thing."

Shit! I hadn't returned Victor Carlson's calls. I could only imagine the explosive anger that was building up in that little S.O.B. if his witnesses were compromised by Armand Backus's lawyers. An unfortunate second thought occurred to me that was even worse. If he lost his witnesses because of my absence, and unavailability for questioning, his rage would be absolutely apoplectic. Either way, I was going to get a Mount Rushmore size ass chewing when I returned home.

"Baby, I don't trust him," Starshine pleaded. "He's acting like he idolizes you, but it just doesn't make any sense. You sent those men to kill him. You sent more to destroy his

The Talking Dog Says

office and they did that awful thing. Why would he still think you're his hero?"

I guess it's a mistake to judge anyone even if some make it awful easy, but I was finding a good deal of respect for Mr. Starshine. He was being a good friend, and giving good counsel. "Oh," replied Backus. "I don't totally trust him either, hon. You know how strange fans can get. They have an idyllic version of their hero and nothing can change that. He or she is like some Godly version of themselves that they cannot ever measure up to. In Mr. Diamond's case, he also smells my money. Surely, you haven't forgotten "Mickey" in Santa Barbara?"

Starshine shrieked. "Oh my Lord, that crazy bitch!"

Backus laughed, heartily. "We've had to deal with this sort of thing forever. I know we can handle our friend, Mr. Diamond. He's just another loser in a long line."

"Pfffftt!" He's no friend of mine, or yours. He knows too much, and he's trying to find out more."

"Please try not to worry. After we finish with him we'll move to Europe like I promised.

Starshine wasn't convinced. "I hope so."

They called it a night a few minutes later. I listened to them chat as they prepared for bed. I took the headphones off and laid down on the bed. No point in wearing myself down, as I'd told Chet, the recorder could be checked, though this late, I suspected they'd sleep until morning.

I fell asleep almost immediately, but my rest was troubled by disturbing dreams that included most of the horror I'd been through in the last few days. Thugs chasing me with automatic weapons. Jackie Midnight singing some Frank Sinatra tune. Apparently, even my subconscious didn't care for the Talking Dog Song. Worst of all, I dreamed about Emily and Kathleen. They were begging me to help them. Hiding behind me as villains bore down on us. Emmie, still alive, pleading for her life as they killed her in front of me. Flashing to Steve taunting me and laughing as he got his hands on Kathleen.

Awakening several times, falling right back to sleep, I continued dreaming more upsetting nonsense. It finally ended toward morning, and I awakened, having just dreamed that Emmie and I were laughing together, and she was assuring me that it had all been a bad dream. Waking up, and realizing that had also been a dream was sad and depressing.

Climbing out of bed, I went to the surveillance equipment, put the headphones on: silence. Good, I had time for a quick shower. The water felt good, and I turned it as hot as I could tolerate. I was thinking about the woman I had heard in Backus's penthouse. It had to be some other acquaintance, and not the Menendez girl. Her disappearance had been headline news in Vegas for months. How do you hide a missing girl from all of your friends, the hotel staff, not to mention the police, who surely nosed around that penthouse during their investigation. I made a mental note to try to question the hotel staff.

When Chet arrived I was back under the headphones. I was tired, but he had dark circles under puffy eyes, and didn't quite look his usual fully enthused self, though he did have his signature grin. "How's it going? Did you get an education tonight?"

"No, but I got an earful of something else in the middle of the night."

"I can only imagine."

"I don't think you can. He had a woman up there."

"Yeah? For what?"

I shook my head. "I don't know. They were in another room. We didn't pick up much, but no mistake. It was a woman. She sounded upset."

"The Menendez girl?"

"I doubt it. How does he keep her from being spotted by the help, or even his friends."

The Talking Dog Says

"Okay, not her. Who then?"

"I don't know. I'm hoping to hear more. Let me know if there's any new development...Starshine did implicate him in the attacks on me."

"Too bad we can never use it."

"I'll figure something out."

"I'm sure you will. Anything else?"

"Mr. Starshine doesn't trust me much. He's very worried that I'm a wolf in sheep's clothing."

"He should see you in your undercover duds...What did Backus say?"

"He thinks I'm a crazy fan trying to get money out of him."

"Good." He motioned at the headphones. "What are they doing now?"

"Having breakfast." I laid the headphones aside, turning the monitor button up so we both could listen.

"I can't believe it," Starshine was saying, amid clinking and clanking glasses and silver. "They really want you to sing!"

Backus sounded happy. "Yes. It's part of a nostalgia show, but they've assured me that I'm to do a complete set."

"Armie, that's wonderful!" the boy gushed. "It'll get us out of here for awhile. I'm so concerned about..."

"Well, I need to talk to you about that."

Starshine's euphoria evaporated. "What?"

Chet looked at me. "He's not going."

"Well, you see..." It was obvious that he didn't want to say what he had to. "You see, Bobby. I need you to stay here and take care of things."

"What! Armie, no!"

"I'm sorry, but you know it would be impossible for both of us to go away right now."

Starshine 'Bobby' began to weep quietly. "Yes. Yes Armie, I know. It- it would be so nice to see you performing again."

Backus sighed. "Please don't cry. It will be filmed, and you can see it then. I'm sorry, Bobby. I don't see a way around it. I'll make it up to you somehow. I always do."

"W-will you finish up this business with that awful bastard before you go?"

"Now, what awful bastard could he be referring to?" Chet laughed.

"Yes," Backus replied. "The taping isn't until the end of the month. I should be able to get Mr. Diamond's money and contract together by tomorrow night. It'll all be over soon, Bobby."

"Contract?"

Backus laughed. "I want to spell out exactly what I expect for my money. Don't worry, I won't put it on paper. I will expect him to be a man of his word; and my dear, you know that I have an ace in the hole to ensure his cooperation should the need arise."

"Yes, I know. I just hope it matters to him."

"It will, Bobby. It will."

"That bastard is evil. He could go all bananas and ruin everything!"

Backus seemed a little annoyed. "Please stop worrying. Mr. Diamond is not the brightest spoon in the silver set."

I turned the sound down. Chet was laughing too loud to hear anyway.

"You know, I don't think either one of them has any respect for me!"

"I think they've got you nailed, James."

"Just for that, you can listen to them all day. I think we're close to something big. What do you make of that 'ace in the hole' business?"

"I think he's full of it!"

The Talking Dog Says

"Maybe, " I said, as I applied the phony mustache to my face, and put on the rest of my disguise, "but he seems to think he's got something on me that's going to keep me in line. I'd sure like to know what it is."

He began laughing again. "He's just feeling cocky because you aren't a very bright spoon, Jim."

I walked out, and could still hear the S.O.B. laughing as I walked down the hall to the elevator.

I slouched through the hotel lobby in my homemade costume. With only a little surprise, I saw the two gentlemen I had seen at my hotel when I checked in. They were standing about twenty yards from the elevators, talking, and didn't appear to see or recognize me. I wanted to confront them, but didn't want to give away my presence in Armand Backus's hotel. I walked right by them to get out of the hotel.

Hailing a cab, I jumped in. "Go around the block and park about thirty yards from the main hotel entrance."

The cabbie turned and looked at me. I was removing my mustache and sunglasses. "I'm following someone. I'll pay you for every second we wait, and a nice big tip if you're a good boy."

"Whatever you say." He moved the car into traffic and zipped around the block until we were soon parked again, waiting. "Hey, you ain't some murderer or something, are you?" he asked, in that kidding way that always has some truth hidden in it. A jackass, a dull spoon, and now I was a murderer: all in one morning.

"No. I'm a private detective."

"No kidding? Like Sam Spade?"

"Just like Sam Spade."

"Wasn't that a great movie? The one about the Maltese Falcon?"

"It certainly was."

"You know," he said. "I think I've seen it a hundred times if I've seen it once." A bigger Bogart fan than I was. Hard to imagine.

"Do you like his other films," I asked. "Bogart, I mean."

"All of them. Whether he was a truck driver, a gangster, or a DA: He was the best of them all."

I laughed. "Yes, he was. Tell me, what's your name."

"Paul Morris." He extended his hand over the car seat.

I shook it. "Hi Paul. I'm Jim. Tell me something, Paul- Do you work this area frequently?"

"Yeah. I take a lot of trips to McCarran and back. I sometimes wonder how many. Thousands, I guess."

"Can you tell me about any oddballs in that hotel?"

"Sure. Half of the people that get in this car are oddballs." I didn't ask him where I fell- I didn't know if my psyche could take more artillery. "Oh, hey! I bet I know what this is about. You're working with the Feds, aren't you? You're working on that goofy half-assed Mafia singer's case!"

"What can you tell me about all that? Is he as bad as they say?"

Paul shrugged. "What do I know? I met him once. He seemed like an okay guy. I know the Feds are after him, and not because he dresses so silly."

"What do they accuse him of doing?"

"Something to do with money. What do they call it when you move money around illegal-like?"

"Money laundering."

"Yeah, that's it; but the big thing is that girl of his what disappeared."

"He had a girl?"

"Listen Jim: I'm a live and let live kind of guy. If he's gay I couldn't care less, but he and that girl sure seemed to be into each other...And you know how celebrities are? They all dress like Martians. Look at Country stars with their ugly hats and frills and spangly shirts. Most of the time they look just as gay to me." Sounded to me like Paul had spent some

The Talking Dog Says

time in the casinos viewing the tourists. "He doesn't usually dress like that," he continued. "Usually he looks pretty good. I guess the mood just sometimes hits him.

"Anyway, she was a nice girl. I had her in my cab a couple of times. She never talked to me like she thought she was special, and I was nothing. I liked her. As a matter of fact, I liked him too."

"Do you think he killed her?"

It took him awhile to respond. "I wouldn't ever suppose about something like that. I know a lot of people think so, but if he did, he put on a hell of an act when she disappeared."

"Really?"

"He was quite upset. He didn't make it through a couple news reports and interviews. Crying, you know. About what you'd expect under the circumstances. Begging for whoever was responsible to return her unharmed. Both my wife and I felt really bad for the guy. I think the Missus even sent him a card- she was more of a fan of his singing career."

"So there's media accounts of all this?"

"Oh yeah. He had interviews on television, and in the papers. Some of the bigger S.O.B.'s even asked him about the rumors and allegations regarding her disappearance, you know, to his face."

Paul sat up straight in his seat. "Hey look! Speak of the devil." He put the car in drive. "Is it him you want to follow?"

Armand Backus, sans his little buddy, was exiting the hotel. A sedan had pulled up and he climbed into it before the paparazzi got to him. He was wearing an Armani suit and looked like a million bucks. If Paul hadn't just said that this was usually how he looked, I'd have almost believed the little speech I had given Backus had done some good. I wondered if he'd taken his new 'Elvis' memento with him. It would be useless until he returned to the hotel, unless, of course, he needed to sign an autograph.

"No Paul," I instructed. "Sit tight. I'm hoping to follow two guys that might be in their keeping tabs on Mr. Backus. Let's wait." I opened my cell phone and selected Chet's number.

"Hey. I'm watching Backus leave. You still picking up anything?"

"Still up and running," he said. "I'm listening to Starshine's singing as we speak. It's hilarious."

"Burn me a CD of that, man!"

"Will do. Are you following Mr. Entertainment?"

"No. Those two mystery agents were in the hotel when I left. I'm waiting to see if I can find out anything about them."

"Good luck."

The two men in question walked out of the hotel a few minutes later. A Camry pulled up a short time later. They tipped the valet and got into the car. I leaned forward, pointing. "Follow the Toyota, Paul."

Traffic was unusually light. I cautioned him not to get too close. In a few minutes we were driving on 3rd Street. It suddenly dawned on me where we were going just before we got there: the Clark County Courthouse. Maybe Agent Burley was right: they were local authorities after all.

The Camry was maneuvering into a parking spot down the street from the main entrance to the courthouse. "Paul, drop me off at the door. Find some place to park. Wait for me." I dropped a fifty dollar bill over the seat.

"You gonna need help with those guys?"

"No. Just relax. I won't be long." I got out of the car. The two men were coming up the sidewalk. I stood , facing them. The taller gentleman saw me first. He paused, ever so slightly, when he saw me. His companion, still looking like a gopher, noticed the other man's hesitance, stopped talking, and looked up.

"Alright fellows, what's going on?"

Gopher looked at Tall and Gaunt. "What do you mean?"

The Talking Dog Says

"Don't dick me around. You were both in my hotel when I checked in. I've also seen you around town. Who are you?"

Tall and Gaunt folded his long arms. "Sounds more like you've been following us. Just who might you be?"

"I might be Mr. Diamond."

"Well, Mr. Might Be Diamond. You might as well be Herbert Hoover for all we care. Where do you get off- accosting citizens on the street." Without another word they walked into the Courthouse. I stood there a minute, thinking, then entered the courthouse. The reception desk was also the security desk.

"I'm meeting two gentlemen. One is really tall; the other, shorter. Have they arrived yet?"

The receptionist smiled a plastic smile. "Mister…"

"Jim Diamond. I'm late for a meeting. I'm in a bit of a hurry."

"I'm sorry, Mr. Diamond. I haven't seen anyone fitting that description. Nor do we have any meeting starting at this time. What were the names of your two gentlemen?"

"Look, I saw them enter just ahead of me."

"I'm sorry sir. You must be mistaken. I'm afraid I have to ask you to…"

"What is this? I saw…"

The security guard rose out of his seat. He was about three times bigger than me, and had that look in his eye like he was about to kick some ass, and make his day. "Sir, you can't even say who it is you're supposed to be meeting. You should just leave now."

"But I saw…"

"We've both been here for at least an hour. No one has come in matching the descriptions you gave," the receptionist said, a little firmer.

It wasn't worth the fight, especially since he was much bigger, itching for a fight, and was removing a large bug zapper from his belt.

"Alright. Alright. I'm going." I left, warmed by the instant looks of disappointment on the faces of both the guard and the receptionist. I tried to retreat with as much dignity as possible, but basically, I turned tail and ran.

It took me a minute to spot Paul's taxi down the street. He was laying back in his seat with his eyes closed. He jumped when I opened the door, but greeted me with a big grin. "How did it go?"

"Something crazy just happened. I followed those two into the building, but both the receptionist and security guard swore they didn't see anyone fitting their description."

"Jim, you've entered the Twilight Zone."

"Get me out, Mr. Serling. I need to make a stop at the Sun."

"You got it." He made a quick turn, going South on 3rd Street to Bonnieville, and then West to Grand Central Parkway. It was only a few miles, and we were there in no time. The Las Vegas Sun: a historic newspaper that had seen everything from Seigel to Elvis, and beyond. I wanted to get a look at anything they had on the Menendez disappearance, and the other investigations into the affairs of Armand Backus.

I was given a warmer reception at the newspaper. Of course, my mission there was much more legit, and straightforward than my long shot invasion of the Courthouse. I looked like a damned fool not knowing the names of the men I was supposed to be meeting. It had been reckless, but I really hadn't had time to weigh the variables.

"Hello, Mr. Diamond. I'm Rebecca Stone. I understand you are doing research on Armand Backus."

"Yes. Thank you."

"As you can imagine," she smiled. "The amount of interest in Mr. Backus has been pretty overwhelming for some time."

"I'll bet it's been quite hectic."

She nodded. "Luckily, that translates into good news for you. You see, we've kept a database file of all the relevant articles- it's up to date as of yesterday. We just didn't have the time or personnel to keep on eye on a room full of researchers. So we gathered everything together and simply hand it out. It costs ten dollars for the copying, Mr. Diamond. I assume that is acceptable."

"Yes, that's fine."

"You don't look like a reporter."

"I'm not."

"Then, you must be either a law man or a lawyer." She leaned forward just a bit. "I hope you haven't gotten the awful task of defending that man."

"No, I'm not a defense attorney." She gave me a wise look, concluding that I was a prosecutor.

"Well, wait here, sir. I'll be right back."

"Do you have any video.? I understand Mr. Backus was quite demonstrative in some interviews after Miss Menendez disappeared."

"No. You'd have to visit the local stations- but we did write about those interviews. Several of them were transcribed for our reporters use. The transcripts we have are included."

"You are an absolute angel, Rebecca Stone!"

She bustled away, and returned with a large packet of photocopied materials. I gave her the ten dollars. "Thank you, Mr. Diamond. I hope you find what you're looking for."

"Thank you."

Paul was talking on his cell phone when I got back to his cab. "Hang on, honey." Then, to me. "Where to now?"

I whispered. "Have I kept you too long? Are you in trouble?"

"No, she understands. It feeds us both."

"I'm hungry. Do you know a good place? Something simple, but good."

"J. Dominicks Steak House," he replied. "Prime rib sandwich that will melt your molars." We pulled up to a plain looking establishment a few minutes later. I invited Paul in to join me, but he was under orders from his wife, and would have a meal waiting for him when he did get home. The building looked old and dilapidated, but the interior was nice. Framed movie star portraits- they were especially fond of Sinatra, hanging plants, and a view of the Strip made it downright charming. An incredibly gorgeous redheaded waitress didn't hurt the décor either.

Paul was right about the sandwich too. As I chewed and watched the waitress, hungrily, I contemplated ordering a half dozen of them, and one redhead to go, but managed to control myself on both accounts, though I could not keep my eyes off of her- her name was Vanessa. Whatever the proverbial "It" was, she was the real deal.

"Come again, honey!" she smiled, as I paid her.

"I'll be back if you're here."

"I'll be here," she replied, quickly writing a note on my receipt. "Tonight, I'll be here."

"Nice to know. See ya."

I walked out of the restaurant with a grin stretched from ear to ear. Back in the cab, Paul laughed. "You look like you enjoy prime rib even more than I do."

"It was good, but the waitress was better." I held up the receipt so he could see her writing.

"Aww, which one? Not the redhead."

"Yes. Vanessa. She gave me her address and phone number."

"Jesus Christ! I've been flirting with her for months. What's your secret?"

"For starters," I laughed. "I'm not married."

"Oh Jim. You're cruel. You're a cruel man...You told her you're a private eye, didn't you?"

"No. I only told you so you'd trust me, and not think I really was a murderer. I hardly even flirted."

The Talking Dog Says

"Life is so unfair. Where are we off to now?"

"Let's go back to the Mirage. I need to make an important call in private."

"Is it about those two guys?"

"Yeah. I have a friend that was in the intelligence field. He'll be able to find out who those two bozos are."

He pulled into the valet parking fifteen minutes later. The meter read seventy bucks. I gave him two twenties to join my fifty in his pocket.

"Thanks Jim." He handed me his card. "Hey, call me if you need me again. Just not tonight...the Missus has plans."

"Thanks Paul. If I don't see you, thanks for everything." I went straight up to my room to make the call. G.H. would likely know if Keyes and Burley were fibbing, and the two mystery men were FBI after all. His wife, Margaret, answered the telephone. "Jimmy! We've been worried. I'm glad you're all right. Hold the line a moment."

G.H. came to the phone an instant later.

"Relieved to hear from you, Jim. Keyes told me that they were backing away from you, waiting for Backus to make his move."

"Yes sir. I think Backus believes I want to extort money from him in exchange for forgetting what he did."

"He could be setting you up, Jim. Dangle a carrot in front of you and then have someone waiting to do the dirty work. It's exactly what he does. He never gets his own hands dirty."

"I don't think so, Herbie. I went to great pain to emphasize my connection to the Bureau. He's smart enough not to make someone else disappear."

"Just remember, he may be smart enough, but is he sane enough. Make sure you have Keyes backing you up."

"They will...if I continue to behave myself."

"She told me about that, Jim. I'd have bet my house, and Mags that your winning personality would grate. It's what they call a sure thing."

"Herbie, there's something else?"

"Yes?" I detected a bit of amusement in his voice, but assumed it was from his assessment of my personality flaws.

"Well, there's two men down here, I'm convinced they're FBI, but Keyes swears they aren't...They were in my hotel lobby when I checked in. They seemed to be keeping an eye on Backus too. Can you check up on them?"

G.H. started to laugh. "Jim, you really need to go back to Detective School. Those are my guys. They're keeping an eye on you for me. I thought, and I still think you're in the middle of a storm, and too proud to take cover."

"I thought CIA couldn't operate on American soil."

"I didn't say they were CIA, Jim. I said, I sent them to keep an eye on you. I was trying to protect you."

"Thanks a lot. Why wouldn't they identify themselves when I confronted them today?"

"I wanted to keep you guessing. I thought you'd be more careful."

"Keyes won't appreciate that. She's been concerned that..."

"I filled Keyes in. She didn't know at first, but I filled her in."

"And she lied to me because..."

"Agent Keyes was just trying to keep you in line. She hasn't had too much success at that has he?"

"Sir?"

"Jim, I have a question for you."

"Yes sir?"

"Burley told me about your present to Backus to gain his trust. A pen?"

Oh Oh.

"Yeah, what about it? I thought it would..."

"A pen, Jim? Are you doing something you shouldn't be doing?"

"I don't know what you mean, sir."

The Talking Dog Says

"Dammit, don't lie to me. I'm the guy that'll end up saving your ass when all this hits the fan!" G.H. cussed. He rarely used profanity-ever. "You are illegally wiretapping that fellow, aren't you? I introduced you to that technology, you think I'm not going to recognize a turd that big when it hits me in the face!"

I didn't dare play dumb or lie again. I said nothing.

"I want you to end it immediately, Jim. Stop it! Now: This very minute. Do you understand?"

"Yes sir, I understand."

"Shut it down. I won't be connected to that sort of thing."

"Thanks Herbie. I understand. Tell me, does the FBI know?"

"No, and I'm not telling them. They don't like you. You'd be toast. Now, go get it done before I change my mind and have you busted myself."

"Yes sir."

Well, Chet would be happy. He was going to be sprung early, and could go back to being a playboy.

I guess I couldn't expect anyone to condone illegal wiretapping, least of all, G.H. who, in his time, may have authorized the very same, and worse; but now retired from formal Intelligence work, he would not be protected by the cloak of secrecy that folds around Agency operations. Chastened by his common sense, and a nagging feeling that I'd let him down, I sat alone in the room, brooding, for close to an hour, before I found the strength to get up and leave for the Mercury Hotel to shut down our Operation.

Hailing a cab- a constant queue of taxis line the entrance to every place in Vegas that is any place, I slumped wearily, in back of the cab. I was utterly exhausted from the stress and exertions of the last few days, and would surely have fallen asleep if it had been a longer trip.

At the Mercury, I climbed out of the cab, paid the driver, and walked into the hotel without my cheesy disguise. I no longer had to worry that G.H.'s men might be Backus's spies or assassins, and if I were spotted by Keyes or Burley at this point, I didn't much care.

Chet was hunched over the receiver with the headphones on. His hands were over each speaker, making sure they didn't slip. "Hey!" I exclaimed. "Guess what you..." He waved at me to shut up. After a moment, he took the headphones off, flipped the monitor switch so we both could hear, a big grin on his face.

A woman was speaking in a spacey drugged voice. "I don't know why you won't let me go."

"My dear, you are my insurance with our friend, Mr. Diamond."

"Insurance? Jim? That's just crazy!" Her words drawled out, lazily. "I just want to go home."

"I am sorry. You'll have to be patient. I give you everything that..."

She raised her voice, still sounding drugged. "You keep me locked up in that stupid little room like a criminal you sick old has-been." We heard a loud slap, and then a second. She began to sob bitterly.

"Starshine, put her away." His voice was angry and annoyed. We could hear her crying and shouting; then again, that strange scraping noise I had heard before, and then nothing.

I looked at Chet. His mouth was hanging open. We both recognized her voice. It was Emily. My Emmie was still living.

"Christ Jim, she's still alive!" Chet said, excitedly. "What should we do?"

I sat down, a hand to my forehead. "I can hardly believe it. She must be in horrible pain- he cut her damned breasts off. The bastard, I'll..." The threat went unfinished. I

The Talking Dog Says

was struggling with my emotions, and not totally succeeding. "I want- I want to run up there and get her out."

"Breaking and entering?" he replied. "There's got to be a better way."

"No!" I stood up. "I want a piece of that S.O.B. I want him to suffer a bit of the torture he's inflicted upon that poor girl."

He shook his head. "Another bad idea, Jim. You can't depend on your CIA buddy to get you out of a string of felonies."

"Yeah, not even wiretapping. I forgot to tell you, I spoke to G.H. today. He figured out what we were doing, and told me to shut it down immediately."

"That's why you're here early."

"Yes. I was stupid to think Herbie wouldn't know. I guess I just hoped all the details wouldn't get back to him, but he doesn't miss much."

"So what do we do? You know, we could just call in an anonymous tip to the police, Jim. They'd have to investigate."

I thought about it, trying to disengage from my emotions. "I can't just pack up and leave it to someone else. Emmie's in danger up there…I could just go up there and ask to see him- all innocent, and once I get inside…"

"I should go with you."

"No. Chet, I need you to clean up this room. If all hell breaks loose, I want our setup out of here. Take it back to the plane."

"Jim, you shouldn't…"

"I can handle myself. Besides, if you go up there, he's going to be suspicious of the extra manpower."

"Do you have your gun?"

"Yes." I touched under my left arm.

"Have it ready, and keep an eye on that little weasel, Starshine. I don't trust him any further than I can spit."

"I will. Look Chet: if I'm not down in the lobby when you get back from the plane, you better call the cops."

He grinned. "That'll be an interesting call."

"Thanks. Hey, here's the key card. Don't check out until you hear from me, and don't bring any girls up here!" I said; kidding.

"I'll try to be good."

"You know I had a a date with a redhead tonight."

"So do I," he responded. "I just haven't met her yet!"

I walked to the South end of the hotel, and into the staircase, which was unlocked. I walked up two flights to the Penthouse level. That door was locked- rich people's privacy apparently trumps fire codes. I pulled my wallet out, retrieving the card Backus had given me. I dialed the number."

"Helloo!" It was my buddy, Starshine.

"Hey, it's Jim Diamond. Can Armie come out and play?"

"Uggghhh," he muttered. "What do you want?"

"None of your business. Just put Daddy on the phone."

"You're absolutely loathsome!" he spat out. "An absolute bastard."

"Look Mary, I don't have much time. Put your boss on the goddam phone."

He sighed, loud, exasperated. "Armand, it's that horrible man. He wants to speak to you."

Backus came to the phone. "Mr. Diamond, must you be so abusive and homophobic"

I laughed at that. "I'm not the least bit homophobic. In fact I have a great deal of respect for your little buddy. He knows exactly who and what he is, and he makes no apologies or excuses. My problem with him is he's whiny, snotty, and has no sense of humor. And he's probably every bit as evil as you are."

"Well, you seem to have it all figured out. Did you call just to share your thoughts today?"

The Talking Dog Says

"No. Actually, I'm in the stairwell. I came to see you, but didn't want to be seen."

"You are still being followed by the FBI?"

"They're all over the place...Now, could you send Mr. Starshine to come let me onto your floor?"

"I have a tremendous urge to make you walk down all eighteen floors and come up like a proper gentleman."

"I'm not a proper gentleman, Mr. Backus."

"Point conceded."

A minute later, Backus himself appeared on the other side of the door. He pushed the door open, and let me in. I had chosen the right staircase, and was only a few steps from his suite. "Ah, now what is this about, Mr. Diamond?" he asked when we were in his suite.

I looked around the room. Gaudy furniture and a complete lack of artistic taste choked the décor. It reminded me a whole lot of my trip to Graceland. It looked like a New Orleans brothel. No sign of Starshine. Apparently, the threat of seeing me was enough to make him disappear.

"You promised me some money."

"Yes. I've almost finished with the details."

"I want to get the hell out of this town, Mr. Backus."

"Are you missing the cows, Mr. Diamond?" It's been amazing through the years: people's perceptions of Minnesota. I either was asked about cows, cold weather, Prince, or Bob Dylan as though they were monuments in downtown Minneapolis that everyone went to and paid homage.

"I want my money."

"The money is about ready. I would think you could be a little more patient, waiting for someone to make you rich."

I took out my gun, pointing it at his head. "I came for the girl, asshole. Bring her to me now."

"Girl? My God, man. What girl could you possibly be talking about?"

"No bullshit, Backus. I will blow your face into pieces...I know exactly what I'm talking about. I know about the girl, and I know there is some sort of hidden room in this dump. Do I have to break the place up to find it?"

"Very well, Mr. Diamond. Follow me." He turned away from me.

Too late, I heard the step behind me. Starshine had been hiding behind one of the ugly sofas. I don't know what he hit me with, but it did the job, and the last thing I remember is my face hitting the carpet, and bouncing. I regained consciousness, I don't know how much later, with a splitting headache. I tried to touch my forehead, and discovered that my arms were firmly tied down. Painfully, I lifted my head to discover that not only were my arms and legs bound to Armand Backus's bed, but all my clothing had been removed, and I was naked.

Big Oh Oh. Not good.

Backus appeared at my side. "Mr. Diamond, it's so sad that it had to come to this. So sad, indeed."

I looked up at him, in pain, and confused. "This doesn't exactly refute the gay rumors."

"So witty to the end. Tell me, how is it that you know so much about my home, sir?"

"I'm a Detective. I have friends all over, in high and low places."

He shook his head. "Once more," he said. "Try telling me the truth."

One might think that in this situation- tied down and in danger of being molested by a madman, I might have been intimidated into cooperation, but I felt the less he knew, the better for me. "I told you. I am a Professional."

He sighed. "That is an incorrect answer." He held up the Liberace pen I had given him. "The correct answer is 'illegal wiretapping,' Mr. Diamond." He gripped the pen like a knife and plunged it into my left shoulder, pushing hard until it had penetrated my flesh about an inch. He stepped back as blood poured out of me. "Guilty!" he shouted, his eyes wide, breathing heavy.

The Talking Dog Says

I screamed in pain. Calmly he covered my face with a pillow until I quieted to gasping and whimpering. He was still furious. His eyes looked possessed, his fists clenched. "You must think I'm incredibly stupid," he hissed at me. "I knew that that pen had nothing to do with Elvis Presley. They're sold in several shops around town, including the Liberace museum. The clip is in the shape of an L, for Christ's sake!" I hadn't noticed that.

"Of course, I just believed you were trying to befriend me, or possibly, gain my trust to aid the authorities. I never dreamed you were spying on me."

"You kidnapped and tortured Emily. I'd have done anything to save her."

"Commendable, but so sad and ironic. Now, you have sealed both of your fates." He took a towel and covered my bleeding shoulder. He sat down on the bed, putting a hand on my chest. "Such a shame you have to die for your transgressions."

My mind was reeling. I was having difficulty thinking straight. I wondered if he had drugged me. I was feeling very drowsy. "Look Backus, you got away with murdering that Menendez girl- you did murder her, didn't you?"

He didn't respond. He was playing with my chest hair with his fingers. "Well," I continued, trying to ignore him. "You won't be so lucky this time. My friend knows I'm up here. He knows I came here to confront you and free Emily. He also knows about your secret room. I'll bet a ton of secrets come pouring out of there. Think about it. My DNA is all over this room. You can clean the blood up, but modern forensics will still find it. Don't be a fool, Backus. Don't ruin your entire life." He clutched a handful of hair, ripped it off of my chest, lifting me off the bed until it gave way.

I screamed. "Goddam it!"

"Armand," snapped Starshine. He was standing nearby, watching. "I told you we should have gotten rid of this bastard the day we met him." He looked like he was enjoying this little torture session.

"Yes," Backus said, quietly. "You were right. It's turned out badly."

"You can still turn it around, Backus. Let me go. I'll do what I can to..."

"No," he said, standing. "I'm afraid it is much too late." He began to remove his own clothing. "No matter what, our lives are ruined, Bobby."

I had a terrible feeling I knew what was going to happen next. "C- come on man. Don't make this something it's not. You're not doing all this because you're a homosexual. You're not a rapist. You're just angry and confused. Step back from the abyss. For God's sake, don't!"

Backus finished undressing, and sat down beside me again. He nodded at Starshine, who began to release one of my legs. Any relief and hope was short- lived when he transferred the leg to a stirrup that was hanging over Backus's bed. "Let me tell you about my childhood, Mr. Diamond." He went back to playing with my chest hair. "When I was eight years old my father molested me for the first time. On my tenth birthday he raped me in a shed behind our house. He told me that if I ever said anything, he would kill my mother and I...After that, it happened so many times I lost count. I felt horrid, and ashamed, but I never said a word right up to the day I ran away...I let him do that to me for years."

"You didn't let him. You were a scared child."

Starshine had just finished wrestling my other leg into a second stirrup. "Yes," Backus agreed. "I was a scared child. You will have to pretend or imagine that part, but I want you to know exactly what happened to me, you judgmental sonofabitch. I want you to know!"

As he put one knee on the bed, there was a loud crash in the other room. Backus jumped back, grabbed up my gun, and went out the bedroom door. A gunshot sounded,

The Talking Dog Says

then several in return. A slug thudded into the headboard of the bed, inches above me, having travelled between my upraised legs to find its mark. Starshine, a look of terror on his face, huddled in a corner, gasping and crying with fright. I knew how he felt. I wanted to do the same. Instead, I did the only sensible thing that I could do, and passed out.

When I regained consciousness, one of G.H.'s glorified baby sitters Wyatt, the tall gaunt man, was looking down at me. My legs and arms had been freed, and I was covered with a sheet to my waist. "Stay still, Mr. Diamond. We've called an ambulance."

"Thanks," I croaked, barely above a whisper. Even to myself, I sounded weak. "It hurts."

"We've stopped most of the bleeding, but you're going to need a surgeon to remove that pen. We don't want to cause any further muscle damage."

"Backus?"

"He's in custody. He's waiting for the paramedics too."

I pushed with my one good arm, laboriously sitting up on the edge of the bed. "He's- he's got a hidden room. He's holding a woman prisoner."

Wyatt nodded. "We found it. She's going to be okay. She's in the next room. The ambulance and police should be here any minute.

I started to get up. "I've got to see her."

"You should sit tight until EMS gets here. You have a serious wound."

I stood up anyway. "I'm sorry. I thought she was dead. I must see her."

"You've lost a lot of blood."

"I'm running on pure 'pissed off' right now anyway." I grabbed my pants off a chair and managed, slowly and painfully, to put them on. Wyatt watched, a bemused look on his face. I stepped past him and went into the living room. Armand Backus was sitting on a chair, with no handcuffs, but he wasn't going anywhere. He'd been shot, with a curious amount of karma, in just about the same spot that he had stabbed me. He was holding a very bloody towel to the wound.

Starshine, dejected and teary, was sitting on a sofa. He had not been wounded, and was handcuffed. "Where are those doctors!" he whined.

"They're on the way up," responded Ogilvie, giving Backus a clean towel. "With the police," he added.

"Mr. Diamond," Backus said. He was looking with some amusement at the pen sticking out of my shoulder, silently wagging up and down as I walked. "Did you want my autograph?"

Before Ogilvie could stop me, I grabbed a handful of his hair, and yanked his head back and forth. "Dogs don't talk, asshole!" I gave him a shove, and despite Ogilvie's best effort, the murdering bastard toppled off the chair to the floor.

"Jim!" I turned: it was Emily. Or a thin, sad version of the beautiful girl I knew. She moved to embrace me, but stopped short, seeing the pen. I held back too. I knew what he'd done to her. She hugged me carefully, and saw me looking at her, a worried expression on my face.

"It was the other girl, Jim. It was her that they mutilated...She was still living when I arrived. Oh God, she suffered so. She died the next day." She pointed at Backus. "That monster had her taken out of here in a giant canvas bag."

"My poor Emmie," I said, caressing her hair.

"Jim, I need to call my mother. She must be sick with worry."

I pulled the cell phone out of my pants- it took some effort with my injury, and handed it to her. I was feeling lightheaded, and abruptly sat down. As she made the call, the paramedics and the police finally arrived.

I found out later how I'd come to be rescued by Wyatt and Ogilvie. Search warrant in hand, they'd broken open the door to Backus's Penthouse, having heard one of my

The Talking Dog Says

screams of pain. Rushing in, they'd been met by a gun-wielding naked man; Armand Backus, who began shooting. Fortunately, his marksmanship was every bit as lousy as his Dog song. Ogilvie, on the other hand had dropped both Backus and Starshine with one shot. That is, the slug had hit Backus in the shoulder, and the mere sight of that had reduced the kid to a crying, terrified mess. He revealed the existence and location of the hidden room in about six seconds.

It was behind a bookcase that had been built over the entrance of a walk-in closet in the bedroom. Emily had been asleep when they found her. Wyatt had carried her into the living room, assuring the poor shocked soul that her nightmare was ended. He had stayed with her until shortly before I regained consciousness. A more macho private eye might be embarrassed or ashamed that he was in the Twilight when all this happened, but I gave myself a break. I'd been cracked over the head with, it turned out, a Grammy Award, stabbed with a really ugly pen, and threatened with rape. Checking out was a gift of mercy I gave to myself.

By the time the paramedics had got to me, I had gone into shock. They immediately gave me fluids, and after getting my blood type, a pint of blood. They saved my life, no doubt, but on a good day I could have walked to the hospital in the time it took them to respond.

Armand Backus spent the next ten days in the hospital, where it didn't seem to matter to anyone that he'd had a shootout with Federal Agents. Wyatt and Ogilvie turned out to be CIA, just not on active duty: a little indiscretion which only G.H. could pull off without seeing the irony of his objections to my questionable behavior.

Never mind that Backus had kidnapped, murdered, mutilated and assaulted nearly a half dozen innocents, the hospital was flooded with cards, letters, and gifts for the former singing star. The stuffed animals- mostly dogs, filled another hospital room and the supply replenished as quickly as the toys could be donated to charity. The sick bastard conducted court from his hospital bed, pledging to prove all the allegations against him were lies, which everyone knew was bullshit, but the cable television networks ate it up for their twenty- four hour news cycles.

How had Wyatt and Ogilvie known to storm the place? Chet: my buddy had packed up the surveillance equipment as instructed, then promptly ran into the two men in the hotel lobby. Knowing they were connected to G.H., he told them that we had discovered that Backus was holding a female prisoner in his Penthouse, and that I'd gone there on a rescue mission. Not being an impetuous Midwestern detective, Ogilvie had called for a search warrant. Chet had managed to give him the impression that we'd gotten the intel from a hotel employee. Gutzy quick thinking considering he was carrying the briefcase with our surveillance equipment.

G.H. must have had friends in the Las Vegas D.A.'s office too. The request was authorized at once. It even included a backdated wiretap order that I'd have to thank Herbie for later. Or, give his ethics lecture back to him. Though the latter was fun to think about, it would never happen. G.H. would know that the Intel came from our surveillance, and not be happy about having to, in the end, pull so many strings to save us.

Burley and Keyes caught up with me in the hospital. Both so angry they could hardly speak to me calmly. Keyes felt I should be prosecuted for obstruction of justice and illegal wiretapping, putting me in a Federal prison for a decade or two. Burley disagreed, wavering between tar and feathers and public hanging.

Inconvenient for either plan; the kidnapping, torture, and murder charges would keep Armand Backus in prison for the rest of his life. Furthermore, the authorities would be able to interrogate Backus extensively, likely getting what

The Talking Dog Says

they needed in their other investigations. All of the above because of me; so they needed me to be on board when it all came to trial. Any prosecution of me would hurt their cases, and I was smart enough to take advantage of it. I would go back to Minneapolis a free man, with FBI blessings, even if it didn't sit right with them.

Emily recovered well, and came to visit me in my hospital room. A couple days of rest had done wonders. She was smiling and joking like old times, but behind it, I could see the remnants of the intense pain and suffering of what she'd been through. It would take a long time to heal those memories, but I was determined to make sure that that happened.

"Do I still have a job, boss man?"

"If you still want it. Your first assignment can be finding us a new office building."

"I'll get right on it." She did, flying back to Minneapolis the next day to be with her family. I'm sure that made Mother Marian happy, but I shuddered to think what she would be saying to Emmie.

I managed a couple of nights alone with a certain redheaded waitress, who, it turned out, was as proficient out of the kitchen as she was in it. She had seen the news reports, recognized me, and forgave me for my earlier noshow. I didn't spend much time worrying about my shoulder. I didn't have to. She took charge, and for once in my life, I did as I was told.

Armand Backus was beginning his tenth day of hospitalization, when two men in surgical scrubs and masks entered his hospital room, implanting two silenced slugs in his chest, and one in his head. He had seen it coming, and had tried to get out of bed, inhibited by his IV attachment. Starshine was safely locked up in jail, trying to make bail, and was spared.

Chet and I were over Nebraska in his plane when the radio gave us the news. It wasn't terribly surprising. For the last six months, allegations of Backus's mob ties and activities had been in the headlines, and leading the news shows in Nevada. The Menendez girl, and then kidnapping Emily had been too much to tolerate for someone in Las Vegas. They had relieved themselves of the burden, and it was so obvious, that even the news media got it right, reporting it as an organized crime retaliation.

Fame being what it is, Armand Backus became a Superstar before they had time to bury him. His old Jackie Midnight recordings flew off of the shelves, and the Dog Song flooded the airwaves again. It topped out at Number 8 on Billboard. Crazed fans with no inclination to acknowledge his dark side, had candlelight vigils and memorials. They gave hysterical interviews filled with tears and manic deification, along with condemnation of his wrongful persecution. They put three of his old hits back in the Top 20 in the same week.

I buried my stereo and television in my back yard.

Chet and I landed at Flying Cloud, just West of Minneapolis. We skidded to a halt on the runway. It had been raining all day and the strip was slick. Chet set the plane down on the only track that hadn't been closed because of flooding. As we taxied across the tarmac to the hangar, I got out of my seat and joined my pilot in the cockpit. Chet looked as weary as I'd ever seen- last minute debaucheries; but, as usual, he was grinning.

"Look," he said, pointing toward the hangar. A lone figure stood waiting for us to arrive. Even covered in rain gear, dripping wet, I recognized Homicide Lieutenant Victor Carlson.

"Carlson. Minneapolis Police," I told Chet. "Methinks I'm about to get a severe tongue lashing."

Chet's grin grew. "Maybe he's just come to congratulate you on helping to take down Armand Backus."

"Not damn likely." We climbed down out of the plane. Carlson wasted no time jumping on me. "You lying little shit, I tried to call you."

"I didn't have any messages."

"Save it. You knew I was trying to reach you. You ignored my calls."

"I was busy capturing the bad guy, Lieutenant."

"You walked out on my investigation, asshole," he snapped. "After promising me you'd do the exact opposite."

"Aw Lieu, you had that mostly wrapped up. Both those guys were falling over themselves to give you testimony."

He poked me hard with his forefinger. "Until you disappeared, you little prick! Backus sent a team of lawyers, and when they couldn't find you, the two perps assumed you'd been taken care of. The both clammed up."

"You didn't…"

"Yes. They made bail. I had to let them go, and they disappeared faster than you did."

"You couldn't…"

Carlson was on a roll. "Well, they did finally re-surface back in Las Vegas, Mr. Diamond. The authorities picked them up this afternoon."

"That's great."

"They picked them up for killing Armand Backus in cold blood!" He was seething now, his eyes on fire. "Which would not have happened if you had stayed home and let me handle this."

"Those two dopes couldn't…"

I got poked again, this time uncomfortably close to my shoulder wound. "They did it right this time. A completely professional hit."

"Backus nearly killed me and Emily. It's pretty hard to feel sorry for the evil bastard." I took a step back to avoid another poke.

"It's not for you to decide, Diamond."

"Look. I..." I wasn't completing many sentences.

"James Robert Diamond: you are under arrest for obstruction of justice."

"You can't be serious."

He handcuffed me. He was serious. It was my first time on the wrong side of the Miranda warning, and I didn't much enjoy it. Chet helped me out by laughing his ass off, until Carlson shot him a look.

"Room in the cell for you too, Fly Boy."

Chet shut up, promised me he'd call my lawyer, then turned his attentions to his airplane so he wouldn't take any further shrapnel.

It was a lonely rainy ride back to Minneapolis. I tried to engage the Lieutenant in conversation, hoping to soften him up, but he was having nothing to do with it. He wrote in his notebook. He talked on his cell phone. His wife was looking for him, but he totally ignored my sorry behind.

Carlson couldn't wait to get me booked. His officers also seemed to be enjoying their duties, as they fingerprinted me, and inventoried my belongings. The Lieutenant didn't move a muscle, stood there, watching the whole time. A faint smile seemed to be growing on his lips.

Finally, they'd finished with me. "He's done," they told their leader, pulling me over to him by my handcuffed hands. Carlson took a hold of one of my arms.

"This way, Mr. Diamond. Your suite is ready." He led me out of the offices, down the hall to the cell block. "Here we are." My handcuffs were removed.

Channeling Arlo Guthrie again, I asked him. "You gonna put me in a cell, Officer Obie?"

"Shut up." He put me in the cell. "Your cute forty year old pop references don't help you in the least little bit, Diamond." I'll be damned. Victor Carlson knew who Arlo Guthrie was.

He slammed the cell door shut. It might be a cliché that that sound brings home the whole experience to a

The Talking Dog Says

person, but it certainly made an impression on me. I could have done without it. "Diamond," Carlson said. "I was also trying to reach you because your sister's man put her in the hospital again. Messed her up good this time. You might want to check on her, if and when you make bail."

I grabbed the bars with both hands. "You S.O.B. Why didn't you tell me? Is she hurt bad?"

He nodded. "We're still looking for Kruckman."

I was stunned. I tightened my grip on the bars, a bit dizzy.

Carlson felt like rubbing it in. "You let her down too."

"You should have told me right away!"

He laughed. "Nonsense. You'd have been impossible. Don't worry, she'll be waiting for you when you get out, but don't expect her to bail you out. She's not too happy with you either."

"She's still in danger if he's loose."

"We have an officer at the hospital until we pick him up. No information is being given out. Even if he calls the right place, he will be told she isn't there."

"How do I get in to see her?"

"When you leave tomorrow, I'll have one of my officers take you over there and introduce you to the staff."

"Thanks. I appreciate that. How did Steve get near her?"

"She left the safe house, Diamond." He turned to go, but turned back. "Oh, and one more thing. We all hope you enjoy our new artwork while you're here." At the end of the hall I heard a burst of laughter.

Looking up, I saw the cause of their amusement. A large poster size blow-up of a photograph had been taped to the wall opposite my cell. It was a picture of me, naked and tied to Armand Backus's bed- the Liberace pen sticking out of my bloody shoulder, and my legs up in the air. No doubt a gift from Wyatt and Ogilvie, perhaps via my soured FBI buddies.

Down the hall, I saw Carlson standing with his officers looking back at me. The hallway was filled with their laughter, catcalls, and rude comments.

My attorney, Aaron Klinesauser showed up that evening. By that time, the poster had been discreetly removed from the wall, but I endured several hours of hilarity before that happened. I didn't even bother to mention it to Aaron. The origins of that poster went back to people I had no intention of annoying with my wounded pride.

"Jim, you surely have a knack for getting on people's wrong side."

"I know, Aaron. Just get me out of here."

"I heard about Las Vegas. Congratulations."

"Thanks, but I'm afraid you're the only person who sees it that way. The two guys that murdered Backus were locked up here, and were released, in part, because I wasn't available to give testimony to their lawyers."

"Yes. I heard the whole story. I talked to Carlson earlier, and I've already had a call from the Las Vegas D.A.'s office, and from the FBI."

"What did they want?"

"Well, they don't like you any better than Carlson does, but they don't want you locked up either." He smiled. "They're afraid that every minute you're in this jail taints your credibility in their very high profile cases. They certainly don't want you to be prosecuted for obstruction of justice."

"Carlson must be furious."

"Maybe, but I don't think he wanted to prosecute you either."

"He came personally to the airport to arrest me."

Aaron smiled again. "He cut some corners by arresting you. It'll never hold up. Now, you know Victor Carlson is too good of a cop to screw up like that. He's much too experienced. He wanted to make his point with you, and then

The Talking Dog Says

send you on your way. As for coming in person, I'm guessing he didn't want to involve any of his officers in that."

"He told you that?"

"No. No, of course not. He did admit, however, that there were problems, and he'd have to let you go. You really did screw him over."

"Yeah, I know. I thought they'd killed my secretary and mutilated her. I had to go to Vegas, Aaron. If I'd have told him that..."

"He's a father, Jim. He understands. Now, I'm going to get you out of this, hopefully tonight. You leave Carlson alone."

"I'll keep my mouth shut."

It got done the next morning. Victor Carlson may have a heart, but he still made me wait while they processed every detail. I expected not to sleep, but I was pretty well exhausted, and slept the whole night. The next morning I was let out at eight a.m. sharp. Carlson's officers were much more subdued seeing me leave. Except for a few hateful glances, they ignored me. Carlson was nowhere to be seen.

Kathleen was at Hennepin County Medical Center, two blocks away on 7th Street. I would have walked, but had to take Carlson up on his offer, if I were going to be allowed to see her. The officer drove me the two blocks to 7th. Thoughts of my sister, tumbled around in my brain. If she was angry with me; well, I certainly was not totally happy with her either. She was bright enough not to leave that Safe House, but as I said before, Steve had his hooks in her for a long time. That discussion would have to wait until she was recovered. Right now, I didn't know for sure what shape she was in.

The officer took me past the Information desk straight to ICU. Another officer was there- that was good, talking to one of their security people. "Danny, this is James Diamond. His sister Kathleen is the one we're watching. Make sure the staff are introduced to him, and he has clearance."

"I'll take care of it right away," the HCMC security officer offered.

In the course of Kathleen's relationship with Steve, I had seen varying degrees of purple shades of injury, but not even the fact that she was still in Intensive Care, or the nurse's quick orientation of her condition, prepared me for walking into her room. Her jaw had been broken and was wired. Her left cheek bone had been shattered. The left side of her face was black and terribly swollen. She was sleeping. "Dear God," I whispered.

"We wired her jaw, but her blood pressure is very high, and we want to stabilize it before we put her in a private room." "Is she in a lot of pain?"

"We're managing her pain with medication."

"Can she speak?"

"She can, but it's difficult for her. She doesn't like how she sounds."

"I think I'll just sit with her awhile."

"Very good." The police guard looked in as the nurse walked out, and turned and went out with her.

I pulled my chair close to her bed, taking her hand in mine, holding onto it. "Oh Kathy," I whispered. I laid my head against her side rails, trying to not cry. I had seen her injured so many times, but this was the worst. I could not believe that any human being could do this sort of a thing to a woman, but knew that it happens a million times a day. It made me sick.

Sitting there, looking at her, my thoughts turned to Steve. I had promised him what I would do if he ever touched her again, and he had half killed her as a response. Perhaps he had taken my threat as a witticism, but I had meant it, and I knew that I would not rest until I settled things with that miscreant of a man. It wouldn't be all that hard to find him, though the police hadn't managed it. I knew him a little better: he didn't have much, if any, money. He had no friends, other than assholes he met in bars, not the best

The Talking Dog Says

mates to depend on when you're in trouble, and trying to stay hidden. They may help you, but they'll give you up for a song in a crack pipe.

He didn't own guns, so I wouldn't have to bulk up my arsenal- the .38 would do fine. He was more or less the stereotypical chickenshit bastard that abuses and destroys women to compensate for his utter failure as a man, and in life. I think guns scared him; but, I reasoned, he might have a knife or two. In a pinch, even his hunting knives would do. If they weren't still in Kathleen's apartment.

Shit! Kathleen's apartment. Surely, the police had checked it, but would they bother posting someone there. Probably not. More likely, they were keeping an eye on the place with regular patrols. Suddenly, I was never surer of anything in all my life: the evil Monster was holed up in their old apartment. There was no reason for him to stay away now. Kathleen wasn't there. He would think that I had no reason to go there. He was wrong.

"Jim," Kathleen said, softly. She had awakened, and discovered her hand attached to mine.

"Hi honey. How are you feeling?"

"Oh you know: like my head exploded."

"I'm so sorry that I was gone. I've failed you."

"You didn't," she said, slow and lispy. "I failed myself, Jim."

"How did he get you to leave that place? You seemed so on top of it."

"He cried like a baby, and begged for me to come back to him. He threatened to kill himself if I didn't..." She started to choke up.

"We don't have to talk about this now."

She continued. "He- he told me that I was the only thing in life that made it worth living, and that he'd learned his lesson. He said he wanted to marry me, and was buying an engagement ring...He knew all the goddam buttons to push, Jim." She wept some more.

I sat with her until she received some pain medication, and nodded off again. The police officer saw me leaving, and held up a hand.

"Yeah."

"Sir, my Lieutenant called. He wanted me to relay a message."

This would be good. "Go ahead."

He cleared his throat. "I'm sorry. It must be a terrible shock to see your sister like this…He said to make sure that you understood that we are looking for the gentleman that did this, and that he wouldn't tolerate you going vigilante and trying something…stupid. I'm sorry. That's what he said."

"Your Lieutenant knows me pretty well. You can tell him I will be looking for Mr. Kruckman, but I will communicate his whereabouts to him the moment I find out where he is. I won't try to bring the bastard in. Tell him I will let him take all the credit for the capture."

"Yes sir." The man was a rookie, and didn't know what that last bit was about, but if he told it to Carlson, he would be acquainted with it swiftly. It was my little revenge for the jailhouse artwork.

Would I ever be done with taxi cabs? The ride home didn't take long, and again I found myself yawning in the back of a car. I paid the driver and went around the back of the house. I hadn't ever had time to fix the front door so I could open it from the outside. I sat down in my recliner; a long lost friend, with a beer. I flipped open my cell phone, and selected Chet's number.

"Hey buddy, did you get sprung?"

"Yeah, just got home…Chet, Steve Kruckman messed up my sister while I was gone. She's at HCMC in bad shape."

"That sucks, Jim."

"Yeah. Well, now I have to hunt him down. I have a check for you, but would you like to earn a little more?"

"What have you got in mind?"

"I've got a sneaky suspicion he's hiding in their old apartment. I threw him out before we left for Las Vegas. I just want someone with me in case all hell breaks out."

"I'll take some more of your money. When do you want to do this?"

"You free this afternoon?"

"Yeah, if it doesn't take too long, or I don't get shot. I'm meeting a woman later."

"Big shock there, Chet."

He showed up at my place packing heat. I had never known him to have a gun, and it looked strange seeing its outline under his jacket.

"You have a permit for that?"

"Oh yeah."

"Since when?"

"Quite some time. I go shooting about every week. I just don't shoot people like you do."

"Chet, if I live to be a hundred, I'll still be learning something new about you."

"I just don't want to be empty handed if Kruckman has gone off the deep end."

"I'm glad you brought it. I'd feel terrible if anything happened to you."

"Yeah," he said, wryly. "You'd have to fly commercial."

"That hurts, Chet." We both laughed. "I doubt he will have a gun, but he might have a knife or razor blade, or something. "

"Should I wait until he stabs you once or twice before I shoot him?"

The apartment that Kathleen and Steve had shared was on Lyndale, North of Lake Street. It was an "Old Minneapolis" building, converted decades earlier into apartments with all the modern conveniences. Now, they had antiquated conveniences and crumbling walls and ceilings. With only Kathleen's salary it was as good as they could afford.

Michael A. Kelley

I pulled my Taurus, a poor car for impressing a woman, but a great car for blending into an average neighborhood, into the alley behind the building. Finding the widest area of the alley, I pulled way over to the side and against the border fence. Chet had to crawl out my side of the car.

"Pull up the hood for me, would you, Chet?" He did. Then, we climbed on top of the car and dropped into the yard behind Kathleen's building. If Steve was there, I didn't want him to see my Taurus, and; if the police came by it would buy me time if they thought that I was having car trouble. I went through my key chain for Katherine's spare keys- outside door and apartment. The back entrance was ill-lit, and a large dumpster sat, stinking in one corner. The entrance was mostly used by buttheads, stepping out to enjoy a smoke. The ground was littered with cigarettes, and children's toys, and the filthy stench of the former, hung heavily in the air.

Chet shook his head, disgustedly. "They wonder why children get cancer, Jim!"

"I don't."

The inside of the building wasn't any less repulsive. Bags of garbage were in a pile by the door, apparently, waiting to mature fully, before being taken out. More toys dotted the floor all the way to the staircase. A stroller with a diaper bag in it was having a contest with the garbage, and winning.

"Lord Jesus," Chet whispered, to my amusement. I doubted that Chet had been in any church since his baptism. "Dude! How could you let her live in this trash heap."

"This was all she could afford, being saddled with that asshole. He works sporadically, and spends her money freely."

"Isn't love a shitty thing."

"Sometimes. Come on, let's get this done."

Katherine's apartment was on the second floor. There wasn't an elevator, and we jogged up the stairs. The second floor halls were not the awful mess that the ground floor was, as if everyone in the building threw their crap down the stairs, or were too lazy to bring it up. Or, the first floor tenants were pigs. I decided on 'all of the above.'

We stopped at her apartment door, listening. I took out my .38. There wasn't a sound coming through the door, but I wanted to be ready. I put the key in the lock, turning back the dead bolt. "Take out your gun, Chet," I whispered. "Wait here. I'll check the apartment."

I opened the door slowly, following my 38 into the room. It was obvious that Steve had been there, even if he was no longer. Drawers were pulled out and ransacked. Cupboard doors were standing open. Dirty dishes and left over food was on the kitchen table. The television and stereo system were missing. I did a quick run through the apartment, knowing he was gone, but having to check. "Come in, Chet. He's not here." Chet came in, and I bolted the lock from the inside. "Just in case he comes back."

Chet looked around the living room. "Kathy doesn't have a television?"

"No. Just the stand. She thought getting an actual set would be pretentious."

"Anything else missing?"

"Stereo too; I'm guessing a whole lot of stuff. That dirty little thief! Kathy said he threatened suicide. Well, I'm going to do everything I can to see that he keeps his word."

"Does she have jewelry?"

I went into her bedroom. Her jewelry box was laying on the floor in two pieces. "Not any more...if he took my mother's rings..."

"Do you think he'll come back if he's cleaned the place out?"

I shrugged. "If he gets hard up for someplace to stay. My guess is he'll sweet talk some unsuspecting innocent in a barroom, and use her for all he can get."

"How long do you want to hang out?"

"Aw- we can go. I will probably check back from time to time."

"Gonna report the robbery?"

"I have to. Steve will take that stuff straight to a pawn shop, there's one right up on Lake he's probably familiar with. We can't do anything without a police report."

The police arrived an hour later. I filled them in on the situation, Katherine's name and whereabouts, and the best list I could put together of what was missing. I didn't know either cop; I was in a different part of town. They didn't know me either, and we all stayed pleasant and professional.

Chet agreed to tag along to the pawn shop on Lake, rather than my driving him home, and having to retrace my path. It was literally just blocks away, in a place much newer than Katherine's apartment building, but was owned by a real pack rat. There was merchandise all over with just enough room to walk around, and no rhyme or reason. A little gnome of an Asian man was the owner. I had met him ten years earlier as a police officer, after an armed robbery at his shop on Franklin. He'd moved, hoping for a better location and circumstances.

"Ahh, Mr. Police Man. A very good man to come to see Ho Che. How are you, Honored Friend." I swear to God, he looked exactly like he belonged on a charm bracelet. He bowed to me, and Chet had to turn away to hide his amusement.

I returned the bow. "Hello Ho Che. You honor me with your graciousness."

"What can I do for Mr. Police Man this fine day. Sun shining in sky. Birds singing in trees…You need new gun? Ho got. How about a present for lovely wife?"

"Neither, thanks." I had told him there was no wife, lovely or otherwise, several times, but had given up long ago. It was just part of his patter. "Ho, do you remember my sister Kathleen? She bought that Central American vase."

"I do remember sister with smile of many angels."

The Talking Dog Says

"Well, her apartment was robbed by her no-good boyfriend, over on Lyndale. Have you received a purchase that included a Toshiba television and a Sanyo stereo, and some jewelry?"

"I have much of those things, but I think I know man that you mean. You come with me, Mr. Police Man: Ho will show you."

"He's hilarious!" Chet said, quietly, so only I heard.

"He told me once that you must give the customer what he wants, and what the customer wants is a good show. He's Chinese, so he gives them what he thinks they want to see. For all I know, he was born in New Jersey."

Chet laughed. "Probably not New Jersey."

Ho poked his head out from the back room. "Get ass back here, Diamond. Damn you, I don't have all day!"

Chet nudged me. "You heard him, Mr. Police Man."

"Well," I said, throwing my arms out from my sides. "You can't expect him to keep it up all the time."

"You might be right. He very well might be from New Jersey."

We joined the great actor in his back room which was a larger version of the confused disarray of his main showroom. "Ho," I asked. "How in God's name do you keep track of where anything is?"

"Place for everything, and everything in place. Ho knows where everything is." He moved to a side aisle and pulled a sheet off of a pile. "Here are things that I buy two days ago from man."

I looked down and saw Kathleen's television, stereo, microwave oven, and even her tennis racket. "Was there any jewelry, Ho?"

"Yes. Ho have it in safe in office. Some very good pieces- look old. Will have to have appraised by expert."

"Did you get his information from him?"

"Oh yes. Very careful to do this. Make photocopy of driving license."

Michael A. Kelley

"You honor yourself with your cleverness."

"Cut bullshit, Diamond. Ho have no interest in going to jail for receiving stolen goods with knowledge. Will clever, honorable Ho be reimbursed for finding belongings of old friend's sister?"

"We'll figure something out," I assured him. "Can I see that driver's license, and the jewelry?"

The bells on the front door jangled. Ho looked at Chet. "You go tell them Ho be right there. Make sure they be honest."

Chet hadn't stopped grinning since we entered the place. "Right away, sir." He turned and went back into the showroom."

"Good man," Ho commented. "Diamond, you don't have lovely wife, do you have lovely husband instead."

"No. No, Ho. We both like girls a lot."

"Ho don't mind gay boys. Why should I? Just cannot make babies that way. No grandchildren."

"Ah, driver's license..."

"Yes, yes, Diamond. Follow me to office of Ho." His office, I was shocked to find, was neat and orderly. It looked better than mine ever had, even before the attack. He saw my surprise. "You like my office, Diamond?"

"Yes, it looks like any top executive could be here."

"That's because I don't keep pawn shop crap in here. Have to keep it nice for visitors. I am important person, Diamond. Don't you forget it."

I laughed. "I won't."

Ho opened a file cabinet and thumbed past a half dozen folders. He reached into one, pulling out a sheet of paper, and handed it to me. "If he has stolen from your sister I hope he lives a life of sorrow and pain."

I looked at the picture. It wasn't Steve. "Marvin Raymond Bailey," I read aloud, copying the name and address into my pocket notebook. "Not the boyfriend, Ho, but I'll

The Talking Dog Says

bet he's someone hired by the boyfriend to sell you stolen merchandise."

Ho had written a phone number on the photocopy. "Ho, is this his telephone number?"

"No! It is number for Marilyn Monroe. She is hiding forty years in Minneapolis. Having affair with Ho!" He roared with laughter, greatly amused to be teasing me. A regular Chinese Chet, he was.

"Can I see the jewelry?"

"Sure thing Diamond." He fished a key out of his pocket and unlocked his small office safe. He handed me a box with every piece of jewelry my mother had ever owned in it. "They belong to sister too?"

"Yes Ho. I'm sorry. I hope you didn't shell out too much for this stuff?"

"Always too much when robbed, Diamond."

Chet was entertaining three very beautiful Chinese girls when Ho and I made it back to the showroom. "Grandfather!" they called, and rushed to his side, planting kisses on his cheeks.

"Girls, girls; I want you to meet esteemed police friend, Mr. Jim Diamond. Mr. Diamond, these are my granddaughters. Ho Ho, Yo Yo, and Kokomo!" His eyes twinkled with the joke.

I looked at Chet who was leaning on a juke box, laughing. The girls, on the other hand, seemed more than a little startled. "Ha Ha Ha Diamond!" Ho laughed. "Old Chinese man make second joke."

"It's official," Chet wheezed, between guffaws. "He's from New Jersey."

"Let's get out of here," I said.

He laughed about it almost the entire way home. "Jim, that's the most hilarious S.O.B. I've ever met!"

When I arrived at home, I found two messages from Emily. The first time, she wanted to know if I was back home. The second time, she had seen a small article in the Tribune about my brief arrest and release. I opened a bottle of wine, as I listened to her voice. I had one glass of the stuff in Vegas with Vanessa, my redheaded waitress friend, and I was feeling thirsty. Flipping open my cell phone, I started dialing my office number, before I realized that no one would answer there. I tried Emily's home number next.

"Jim! Are you okay?"

"Yes, I'm fine. How are you doing?"

"You know, it's hard, but I'm glad to be home. Mom's being sweet. She doesn't want me working for you anymore, of course. She won't come out and forbid it; she knows I make my own decisions, but she's not happy."

"I feel for Marian. She's only looking out for you like a mother does."

"I know. She's actually been reasonable considering I was kidnapped and held prisoner by a madman. If I had been seriously injured…Are you really in trouble over all of that, Jim? Will you have to…"

"Aaron's confident it will go away. Prosecuting me is apparently not in anyone's best interest. It will damage my credibility on the witness stand."

"But Backus is dead."

"Yes, but my work out there will convict at least a dozen other people, including Mr. Starshine. You don't build a money laundering operation all by yourself. They're hoping to get Starshine's cooperation too, and with Backus gone, I'm sure they will."

"I had several conversations with him. He's from a completely average family in Nebraska. His real name is Robert. Did you know that?"

"Yeah. Starshine seems to suit him better."

"Look Jim, I have to run now, but I wanted to tell you: I think I found a new office site for us: great location in Golden Valley. When do you have time to take a look?"

The Talking Dog Says

"Emmie, there's one other thing I need to tell you. Steve put my sister in the hospital while I was in Las Vegas. She's still there."

"Oh Jim, I'm sorry."

"He's in hiding. I'm on his trail, but I can take some time off tomorrow morning. Maybe stop over and pick me up about 11 a.m.?"

"Okay Jim. I'm excited for you to see this place...but please say hello to Kathleen for me, okay?"

"Sure." I hung up, then called Information, and got connected to the Minneapolis Police Department. "Robbery Division, please...Hello? This is Jim Diamond. I reported a robbery at Lyndale and Parker. Well, I've tracked down the stolen goods to a pawn shop: 'Ho Che's Mini Pawn Shop' on Lake Street. Mr. Che has agreed to hang onto the stuff. You might want to send someone over. What? Richardson. Thank you Sergeant. You'll put him onto this? Thanks again."

Now, I would have to let Katherine know what had happened at her apartment. I didn't want her to find out from the police, and it would help to know her belongings had been found. I live off University and 8th Avenue North. I drove down University to Hennepin, and cut over to the hospital, passing my favorite wine shop on the way. Minneapolis is a relatively small community, and easily travelled at non-peak hours; but rush hour is a bit of a nightmare, despite the light rail. I had wished that Chet owned a helicopter on more than one occasion.

Kathleen was awake and feeling better. She was eating her dinner when I was escorted into her room. She took the bad news well, the likelihood of it happening, probably as obvious to her, as it seemed to me. "Did he take Mom's jewelry too?"

"Every bit of it, but I found that too."

"That asshole," she said, slowly, but with fire. "I hid it so he couldn't ever find it. He knows how much it all meant to me. You are going to get him, aren't you Jim?"

"Yes. He had an accomplice pawn the stuff, and the guy had to leave his information on file. If Steve is staying with him, I'll have him. If he's not, the guy may want to co-operate."

"Thanks Jim. Give him a kick in the ass for me."

"It'll be my pleasure, Kathy."

"How is Emily?"

"I talked to her earlier. She seems to be doing okay. Marian's with her. Don't ask me how she is, I don't know."

"Marian would be better off if she could forgive you."

"I never gave her anything to need to forgive me for."

It's probably not very easy to smile with your jaw wired, but Kathleen managed it. "Two things Jim," she said through wired teeth. "You became as close as a father to Emily as she's ever had; and more difficult for Marian, she never has stopped loving you."

"Come on! They've got you watching too much day-time television."

"Laugh if you want. She loves you, and you have no need for her whatsoever. Men are so…"

"Kathy! The three or four times we've spoken she's been snotty and resentful. This last incident can only fan her distaste. I put her daughter in harm's way."

"Has she called you and told you that?"

"No. We haven't spoken about anything for a long time."

"Call her once in awhile, Jim. Let her know it matters to you how she feels…Don't get me wrong, the relationship is gone, but you can still get past snotty and resentful."

"I don't know…"

"Jim, I'm tired. Go out and find Steve and cut his nuts off for me. Tell the nurse I'll be needing a better office if I'm going to be doing family counseling." I smiled as I walked out. She was going to be all right.

Mr. Marvin Raymond Bailey lived in an apartment above a bar on Lyndale. The XYZ Club; about ten blocks from

The Talking Dog Says

Kathleen's apartment. A favorite watering hole of Steve's, it was likely that the two scumbags had met there, and adjourned to Bailey's upstairs room for some heavy drinking, and planning the robbery. I entered the bar through a back entrance. It was one of those places that has no overhead lighting turned on. Little electric candles punctuated each table and booth, and additional lighting on the walls did little. A good hangout for a thieving, woman- beating bastard to hide. I walked slowly past each booth, but didn't find Steve, or anyone who resembled the license picture in Ho's file cabinet.

I stopped at the bar. "I'm looking for a friend. Bailey. He lives upstairs."

The bartender looked at me intently. "You a cop?"

"No. I owe him money."

"Hey, that's good! He owes *me* money. Can you pay him in front of me sose he maybe feels a little inclined to pay me?"

"I'll make sure he does. How do I get up to his apartment?"

"Stairs in the front entrance. Ain't no number on his door, but he pasted a Harley-Davidson sign on it. The other room is his storage area."

"Is he home?"

"Don't know. He comes and goes. He's usually down here after nine."

I wanted to ask him about Steve, but didn't want to arouse any suspicion. "Thanks. If you see him, let him know I have his money."

"I'll do that, mister."

I went to the front entrance, found the stairs, narrow, and quite dusty. I went up the steps slow and careful, listening. At the top of the staircase, I found a small landing. The apartment door straight ahead, the storage room next to it, and that was it. What surprised me was the strong smell of Lysol disinfectant. The wood wainscoting, and both doors had been cleaned meticulously. The odor was rather overpowering in such a small space.

Putting my ear to the apartment door, right over the motorcycle decal, I listened. I couldn't hear any music, voices, or television. I rapped loudly, but no one came to check the peep hole, and no one opened the door. I trudged back downstairs, popping in to see the bartender. "He isn't home. What's with all the Lysol disinfectant?"

"Ack. He's a huge clean freak. Didn't you know? He's always scrubbed and perfumed, and he cleans that landing every single week. I used to think he was just blocking out the cigarette smell from down here, but now we don't have any smoking. He's just a clean freak. He buys that Lysol stuff by the case."

"I'll try back later. Thanks again."

It was rush hour now, and Lyndale was bumper-to-bumper traffic. I eased the Taurus into traffic, and had to go south a couple blocks. I took a left against the oncoming vehicles, and a moment later heard frantic horn blowing. I looked in my rearview mirror. Behind me a white Lexus had followed me across Lyndale, and apparently cut it too close for an oncoming driver's comfort. The car made it across Lyndale unscathed, but judging from the horn and squealing brakes, not by much.

I went around the block, turning back on Lyndale, heading North. I was hungry and thought a quick stop at Rudolph's would be nice, and would eat up time before I had to go back to the XYZ to check on Mr. Bailey again. Unfortunately, half of the population of Minneapolis had decided the same thing. I walked in the door, saw the crowd waiting, and walked back out. I had no choice. I had to go home. Late night, it seemed, was the more likely time to catch the pair of rats I was after.

Lyndale became Hennepin, and I retraced my path through downtown to get to University. It was less than ten minutes from Rudolph's and it took nearly an hour. When I did get home, once again, I had to use the back door to get into my own house. I absolutely had to get the front door fixed. I called Emily. "Hey, it's me. If you're up to it, I have a work assignment for you."

She giggled. I'll be seeing you in the morning."

"Yeah, but get on this bright and early. My front door is still busted from the home invasion. I have to lock it from the inside and then go out the back door. Take care of it, would you? I'm up to my neck trying to be there for Kathleen, and hunt down her dumb ass boyfriend at the same time. If you're not up to it, I understand. I feel bad I'm not giving you more time."

She laughed again. "Oh Jim, you had me at 'work assignment.' "

"Thanks. I'll see you at eleven sharp tomorrow morning."

I was standing in my living room, looking out the picture window, as I closed the cell phone. A chill ran up my spine: a white Lexus was slowly cruising by my house. I strained to see the driver, but the windows were tinted. If it had gone by the house at regular speed, I'd have thought it was one of those crazy coincidences that pop up from time to time; but not when it was obviously checking out my place. Not after everything that I'd just been through.

I didn't get much of a nap. My mind was rehashing the last two weeks, freshly primed by the mysterious Lexus that was following me around town. I knew it probably wasn't Steve or Marvin Bailey. The two of them together didn't have the credit to rent a Lexus. I doubted even Steve was dumb enough to blow every cent Ho had given him for a first rate rental car.

Of course, it was Steve I was thinking about: I couldn't count on him to do the rational or common sense thing. He was an idiot, but he was very good at manipulating people for whatever he could get out of them. He might just fancy using a Lexus to dupe some poor soul into trusting him. I silently resolved that if it was him stalking me, I would fulfill my promise of introducing his intestines to my gun.

I arrived back at the XYZ Club just before ten o'clock. The place was packed. A few more lights were on, but it was still dark inside. I spotted Carl the bartender, now sitting on the customer side of the bar eating a burger, and drinking beer. "Hey," he said, as I sat down on the stool beside him. "Back again? Did you talk to him?"

"No, I just got here."

"Well," he said, wiping his mouth with a napkin. "He's right over there in that booth. The one with the blond cutie."

"Thanks." I got up, putting a ten dollar bill next to his plate. "The burger is on me, and I will ask him to pay you."

I walked over to the booth. Marvin was about five foot nothing. His dark hair hung down over his eyes. His teeth were in sad shape. He was thin, but it did look like he worked out. His arms were buff. I surmised he knew how to work if he had to. "Hey, Bailey. We need to talk." I slid into his side of the booth, pushing him to the wall. I looked across the table at the 'blond cutie.' She was young. No way she was twenty-one. Marvin was trolling for the vulnerable just like Steve did.

"Honey," I told her. "He doesn't have any money. He steals from women his buddy Steve has put in the hospital, and then sells those stolen goods at pawn shops. You look like a decent kid. You should get as far away from this little prick as you can get!"

"You stupid fucker!" he blurted out. The girl, without a word, jumped out of the booth, looking at him like he was every bit the shithead that I believed he was, and disappeared out the front door.

"Who the hell..." he started to say. I punched him in the side. He groaned, slumping, and sucking for air. I moved over to the other side of the booth.

The Talking Dog Says

"Marvin, you pawned all my sister's things the other day. I believe that your friend Steve put you up to it, but I'm still pretty pissed at you anyway. Tell me where Steve is."

"I don't know. He's not my friend. He's just a guy that drinks here. He needed a favor. I was broke, so I helped him out."

"So you didn't help rob my sister's apartment."

"No. No, he told me that he was moving, and had warrants out for him. He didn't want to give his identification at any pawn shop, but needed to get rid of his belongings to have enough money to go."

"I'll choose to believe that, Marvin; but you're going to help me find him."

"I don't want to help you do anything. Screw you and your stupid sister."

I slapped him hard. He sat there, shaking with hurt and rage, too stunned to even get up and run. "I could just call the police, Marvin. I'm guessing they'd look into things a little deeper than I will. All I want is Steve Kruckman."

"Don't call the police. I'll help you. He met some chick in a bar across the street. A big boned whore named Nadine. She guards a corner at Lake and Chicago. She may know where he is."

"You're not just jerking me around?"

"No. No. He hasn't been here since I did that thing for him. I just figured he had taken off like he said he was going to." He put a hand to his face. "You didn't have to hit me."

"Call the police, Marvin. Tell them this guy hit you because you sold his sister's stolen belongings to keep yourself in crack for the week."

"I don't do drugs either."

"No, you're a Lysol inhaler, Marvin."

He shook his head. "It smells clean, and it keeps the bar smells out of my room. Look, I didn't know anything about your sister."

"Well, I'm going to go looking for Miss Nadine. If you're lying to me, I'll be back."

"I'm not lying. He was real interested in her."

"We'll see...Oh, and Marvin: pay your damn rent."

It was only a couple of jumps to Chicago and Lake, a lovely place to visit at any time of day, but even more peachy after dark. I spotted the girl- the biggest girl of her pursuits I had ever seen. She was six feet tall or more, not necessarily overweight, but nevertheless, a daunting figure of a woman.

I parked up the street from her, waiting. She strolled over in a few minutes, leaning on the top of the driver's side door. "Date, honey?"

"I'm looking for someone, Nadine. I'm willing to pay you for information."

"I don't know anyone." I laughed to myself. That was probably more intensely honest than she had intended to be.

"His name is Steve. Tall and thin. Ugly mustache."

"Oh him. He likes to beat up women?"

"Yeah, that's him. He put my sister in the hospital, Nadine."

"Ain't seen him in a couple days. He tried that shit on me! Can you believe it? He didn't have any money and thought I'd be all afraid of his ass cause he's a man. He hit me right here." She touched the end of her chin. "Expected me to fall down too- you know what I did? I picked him up and threw him just like one of those professional wrestlers." She laughed, a loud genuinely funny laugh. "He screamed like a little girl on a roller coaster. I never seen anything so funny."

"Any idea where he is now?"

"He's got a friend on Lyndale- lives above a bar. He was staying there."

The Talking Dog Says

I handed her a twenty and my card. "If you see him again, would you call me. There's a hundred in it if I catch up to him."

She pocketed the twenty- that is, she stuffed it into her cleavage. "I'll do that, mister. You sure you don't want a date?"

I laughed. "Thanks Nadine. Some other time: I'm looking for another kind of pussy tonight."

She started laughing again, and I drove away. Nice girl. I liked her. She could probably break every bone in my body if she was so inclined, but I liked her. I'd have given just about anything to see her kicking the shit out of Steve. Now, I had to go back to see Marvin again. The little sonofabitch probably had Steve holed up in his apartment. If he wasn't still there, Marvin would be facing some grim consequences.

It was just shy of Midnight when I climbed the stairs to Marvin's apartment. I stifled a cough from the Lysol smell, and listened outside the door. I heard pots and pans rattling. I took out my .38 and tried the doorknob. It was locked. I considered knocking the door down, but decided to knock instead. I held the gun behind my back.

I heard the deadbolt click, and the door opened a crack. One of Marvin's eyes peered out, recognized me. "Oh Christ! You!" I threw myself into the door before he could slam it shut, charging into the room behind my gun. Marvin had fallen to the floor, but he jumped right back up. He looked absolutely crazed and wild, and for the first time, I saw he was holding a large meat cleaver. No sign of Steve.

"Put it down, Marvin." I pointed the gun at his face. That usually promotes immediate compliance. It didn't this time. He stood there, gasping for air; sweating profusely and shaking like a leaf. "Marvin, put it down. I'm not telling you again. We can talk about this, but put the goddam thing down."

He seemed to think for a moment, still shaking, then with an abrupt cry, raised the cleaver and jumped toward me. I shot him in the chest twice. He flew backward from the impact, but the meat cleaver twirled wildly forward, whirling inches from my head, into the hallway. I kept the gun on him, wondering why the hell he had completely lost it over a bad pawn shop deal.

He was dead. I put the gun away, and flipped open my cell phone to call in the shooting, careful to mention the meat cleaver wielding psycho that had attacked me. Police on the way, I started to look around. I opened a window- despite the Lysol, Marvin's apartment had a funky smell happening. Then, remembering that I'd heard him rattling pans, I went into the kitchen. Perhaps Marvin was into some exotic foreign cooking.

A frying pan was sitting on an unlit burner with a large chunk of meat in it. "Oh my Lord," I muttered, recognizing a human heart when I saw one. On the next burner was a pan of what looked like intestines. I leaned weakly against the refrigerator, then; as if in a dream, opened the freezer door. The scream choked and gurgled in my throat. I jumped back, pushing the pans on the burner to the back of the stove.

In the freezer, Steve, or at least his head in a large freezer bag stared back at me. When I jumped , Steve shifted, rolling out of the freezer compartment, smacking the floor, and rolling toward the living room. It was much too late for him to escape, but God bless him, the sonofabitch tried. The freezer compartment was full of packages.

I stumbled out of the apartment, stepping around the head to get away; scared shitless, horrified beyond words, and very close to vomiting. I collapsed at the top of the stairs, hanging onto the hand railing to keep from falling down the entire flight. The police arrived few minutes later. I just pointed them into the apartment and sat there, weak

The Talking Dog Says

and still nauseous. An officer came back out of the apartment. "Sir, you walked in on this?"

I nodded.

"Are you carrying a weapon?"

"Yes. Here." I pulled my coat aside, and he reached over and took it out of the gunbelt with two fingers, dropped it into an evidence bag.

"We're going to have to take you in for questioning."

"You're arresting me?"

He looked at my driver's license. "No sir, Mr. Diamond. At least, I hope not. As long as everything is as it seems. It's pretty obvious what was going on here, but crime scene is on their way. We need you to tell us everything."

"Sure. I can do that right here."

"This is going to be a very crowded place in about ten minutes. We want to get you out of here before the media arrives."

He was right. I got up. He walked me downstairs and put me in a patrol car. A minute later, another officer got in. A van from one of the local television stations pulled up as we left the scene. I was glad to avoid that chaos.

I sat in an interview room for thirty minutes. I couldn't have fallen asleep in my own bed, but I was so exhausted, I bent over the interview table and closed my eyes. I sat up when the door opened and two detectives entered. They sat down on either side of me.

"Thank you for coming in so late, Mr. Diamond. We realize you've been through a lot tonight, but we need to get your statement.

"I understand."

"Just go ahead, if you will sir. We'll have questions when you're done."

I told them the whole mess from discovering the robbery at Kathleen's apartment, finding the stolen merchandise at Ho's shop, and how that led me to Marvin Bailey- something, by the way, that Robbery Division could have done if they'd bothered to follow-up on my report. I laughed, telling them about my trip to see Nadine the Hooker on Bailey's tip, and how that led me back to a serial killer, preparing to make Steve his midnight snack. The only detail I fudged was my entry into the apartment. I knew the evidence wouldn't contradict that Marvin had let me into the apartment of his own free will, albeit, with a meat cleaver in hand. Forcing my way in would only cloud the issue- though, if the crazy bastard had lived, it probably would have gotten him off on a technicality. It's a ridiculous world sometimes.

A very tired looking Victor Carlson walked into the Homicide Division as they were preparing to drive me back to my car. I thought he'd be annoyed with me after the message I'd asked the HCMC police guard to relay to him. Instead, he shook my hand and told me the city was in my debt. He'd been at the crime scene; and, it turned out, early examination of the contents of Marvin Bailey's refrigerator included the body parts of as many as eighteen persons. Conveniently, Marvin had dated and named the freezer bags.

"We may clear over a dozen homicide and missing person cases throughout the country, Diamond. If that happens, I'll put you up for Commendation myself."

"Thanks Lieutenant, but I just lucked out."

He shook his forefinger at me, but didn't poke me this time. "You did good solid detective work. The luck is that he isn't feasting on *your* intestines . Now, go home. Get some rest. If we need anything further we'll let you know."

"My piece?"

"We'll have to keep it for now. You'll get it back."

I nodded. "Good night Lieutenant. Thanks for the kind words."

"Oh, and Diamond. Thanks for not trying to bring Kruckman in by yourself. I like a man who keeps his word in the end." He was actually grinning.

The Talking Dog Says

"It would have taken me all night to put him back together again!"

By the time they got me back to my car, and I drove home, it was four a.m. I wearily collapsed in my recliner and fell asleep. It was a fitful bit of sleep, filled with Marvin Bailey, and Steve's head rolling around. I awoke at ten, with the remnants of a dream of using Steve's head as a bowling ball. I was more rested than I had hope of feeling, but I didn't feel much like going anywhere. It was much too late to cancel my trip with Emily, so I'd have to suck it up and get motivated.

I jumped in and out of the shower, dressed in Olympic time. I went into my closet for my spare gun, a Smith and Wesson 45. I was feeling a little jumpy, and in my profession, you feel naked without a weapon. The Tribune was waiting on my front step, and I looked at it sitting outside in a light cool breeze, waiting for Emily. They already had the story: "Grisley Murders Discovered: Killer Dead." I liked the sub-title: "Local Hero, a Hero Once More." I read the article, wondering, the further I got into it, how they'd gotten every detail so quickly. The answer was Victor Carlson.

> "Investigating an assault case Wednesday night, Minneapolis private eye, James R. Diamond, of the Diamond Agency, discovered a horrific multiple murder scene in the Whittier neighborhood. His investigation uncovered human remains of more than a dozen victims, including his assault suspect. Alleged serial killer, Martin Raymond Bailey, 27, of Minneapolis was shot and killed by Diamond in a confrontation at the scene.
>
> No stranger to murder cases, it was James Diamond who investigated the cold case murders of Anthony Peters Cochran and Jessica Kelly Daniels in 2006. He identified and arrested a suspect, Michael Roy Greene, who was later convicted of both murders and

is currently serving two life sentences without parole in Stillwaterprison.

Only last week, Mr. Diamond returned from Las Vegas, Nevada where he assisted the FBI in their investigation of former singing star, Armand 'Jackie Midnight' Backus, who was facing kidnapping and murder indictments, before his assassination in Las Vegas. That investigation is ongoing in Nevada.

Minneapolis Homicide Lieutenant Victor Leslie Carlson credited Diamond in the Bailey case for his contribution to the community. "His investigation stopped a bloody rampage that stretches back several years, and saves the lives of new victims. Mr. Diamond also saved this department, and the taxpayer, thousands of dollars." Lieutenant Carlson also added that he would personally nominate Mr. Diamond for high commendation.

The police investigation of the murder scene, and of Marvin Bailey, continues.

"Leslie!" I laughed. I'd have to throw that into a conversation someday. Carlson had made certain that his department did not unjustly take credit for the arrests. I sat on my front step, a little stunned, a little amused. The newspaper article alone would put the Diamond Agency into the national news. It was more important than ever that I get an office up and running.

Emily arrived a few minutes late. I climbed into her Honda with the newspaper. She lunged at me, hugging me tightly. "Oh my God, Jim! Oh my God! You could have been killed, you silly bastard!" Her hands were shaking, and tears were streaming down her face. She had already seen the newspaper.

"Emmie, I better drive."

"No, I'm okay." She moved back in her seat, dabbing at her eyes with a handkerchief. "I just can't believe it, Jim. Take a day off, for Christ's sake!"

The Talking Dog Says

I laughed. "Believe me, I wasn't looking to solve a multiple murder, but it sure is going to be good for business."

"Have you watched the television this morning?"

"I didn't have any time."

"Jim, the National news is running with the story. You are going to be mobbed very soon. We've got to get this office thing settled."

The location she had picked out was an office building alongside a strip mall in Golden Valley, east of Hwy 169. A young woman, standing in front of the building, waved at Emily.

"Jim, this is Candy Lewis. She'll show us the suite."

The suite had three large rooms, and a cubbyhole kitchenette with a refrigerator and a microwave oven. Coming prepared, the efficient Ms. Lewis had a two year lease prepared, and I signed, knowing that my business was about to go through the roof. I immediately began fantasizing a staff of two or three investigators, and a company president sitting around, reading paperbacks and drinking wine. Excited by the prospect, I checked the 4th Floor view, and saw a white Lexus pulling into a space two spots behind Emily's Honda. The hair stood up on my arms.

"Sonofabitch!" I whispered, alarming both women.

"Jim, what is it?" Emmie came to my side at the window.

"I don't know. See that white Lexus parked behind your car? It's been following me around since yesterday."

"Call the police."

"You do that. I'm going to get this settled."

I walked out the front door, my 45 held at my side. I walked briskly toward the Lexus. Behind the tinted glass I saw movement. The driver's side door opened. A slim masked figure jumped out, pointing a nine millimeter at me. I fired, shattering the windshield of the Lexus, then fired again, hitting an outstretched arm. My attacker went down, dropping the gun, screaming and cursing loudly.

I put away my 45, grabbed the masked figure and lifted him or her onto their feet, and up against the hood of the Lexus. With my free arm I pulled the mask off.

I gasped in surprise. It was Starshine. "You asshole! You horrid asshole!" he exclaimed, trying to cover the bleeding hole in his arm.

"Mary! What are you doing here?"

"Oh, I hate you. I hate you. I hate you," he ranted. "You killed Armie, you bastard. You took him away from me!"

"Bobby," I said. "His own mob ties killed him."

"You caused it, and you were so cruel to him. You said such cruel things to both of us."

"What did I say?"

He was both livid and seething, and it's probably a sin that I was so entertained by it. "When he was sitting there bleeding: you told him that dogs don't talk! You told him that when he could have been dying. What a thoughtless, horrible thing to say!" He wept.

I laughed at it. "That's it, Bobby? That's the reason you've jumped bail to try to kill me?"

"You bastard!"

"As I recall he had just made a snotty remark about the pen he'd implanted in my shoulder. Not to mention that if the Feds hadn't arrived you both would have raped me; and I'm the one that's out of line! You're one crazy fucked up dude, Starshine."

He began struggling, dancing on my arm like a spastic marionette. I doubted I'd need to rap this one with my gun, so I just whacked him in the side of the head with my fist. He went down, whimpering, and I handcuffed his arms behind his back.

The police arrived and took charge, confiscating another gun. I explained who Starshine was, and that he was a fugitive from Nevada. They took a full statement and released me. Emily held onto me the whole time, shaken up by the experience, but relieved that I hadn't been injured.

The Talking Dog Says

"Jim," she said. "This kind of stuff has got to end!"

I laughed softly. "Yes. It has to. I'm out of guns." I saw the newspaper sitting in her car. "Sadly, honey," I added. "This is probably only the beginning."

Made in the USA
Charleston, SC
21 June 2012